Books & Broadswords

VOLUME ONE

ALSO BY JESSIE MIHALIK

The Consortium Rebellion Trilogy
Polaris Rising
Aurora Blazing
Chaos Reigning

The Rogue Queen Trilogy
The Queen's Gambit
The Queen's Advantage
The Queen's Triumph

The Starlight's Shadow Trilogy
Hunt the Stars
Eclipse the Moon
Capture the Sun

Starlight's Shadow Stories
Honor and Shadows

BOOKS AND BROADSWORDS

VOLUME ONE

JESSIE MIHALIK

BOOKS & BROADSWORDS

Copyright © 2024 by Jessie Mihalik

Ebook ISBN: 9781641972833

KDP POD ISBN: 9798325015991

IS POD ISBN: 9781641972895

NYLA Publishing

121 W 27th Street, Suite 1201, NY 10001, New York.

http://www.nyliterary.com

For my brother, who sparked the idea
And for Dustin, my love

ACKNOWLEDGMENTS

This book wouldn't exist without my brother, who gave me the idea for the initial story. I tried to get him to write it himself, but when he refused, I wrote it for him. I hope you enjoyed it, baby bro! <3

Thanks to my fabulous agent Sarah Younger and the whole team at NYLA for doing the hard work of turning a story into a book.

Thanks to my husband for his endless support. Love you!

And thanks to you, dear reader. It's because of you that I get to do this job I adore!

These stories were originally posted as a serial on my blog, www.jessiemihalik.com, and they are largely unchanged, but I've included a new bonus epilogue as a thank you for purchasing the book. If you wished the romance was open door, this epilogue is for you. If you didn't... well, maybe skip it. :)

BOOKS & BROADSWORDS

CHAPTER 1

I set the royal mark on the counter, and the merchant's eyes glowed, first with greed, then regret. "I can't make change for that," he murmured, his gaze on the gold coin. "You'll need to go to the bank."

"I don't want change," I replied quietly, trying to keep the barely contained excitement out of my voice. "I want *books*."

The merchant laughed and swept an arm toward the corner of the shop I'd already perused. "You could buy every book I own, and I'd still have to make more change than I have. Go to the bank."

"I will take them all. Use what's left to pay off the balance of whoever needs it most."

His eyes widened. "You're serious?"

"I am. I made a list of the copies I want. Do you have boxes I can use?"

The merchant nodded and hurried off to find some empty boxes before I could change my mind.

He took the gold coin with him.

I moved to the shelves and started making stacks of books. When he returned with two large crates, we loaded books into them with quick efficiency. He helped me carry the first crate outside to my waiting handcart. He frowned at the cart and slid an assessing glance over my slight build.

He shook his head with a quiet sigh. "You won't be able to haul all of this by hand, but with the change you're owed, you can buy a pony and wagon. Wait here, and I'll get someone to find one for you."

I stopped him with a hand on his arm. "No need. The cart has a clockwork-assist. I will be fine, but I appreciate the offer."

The merchant looked skeptical, but he helped me load the rest of the books without a fuss. He watched me pull the cart away, easy as you please, and his worried frown morphed into a smile as he waved. "Thank you! I'll have more books next month, if you're interested."

"I'll check in the next time I'm in the area," I assured him.

I passed a few people on my way out of town, but none of them paid me any mind. The road was empty and the sun was warm, so I made good time. It was midafternoon when distant hoofbeats broke the silence.

The rider was pushing their horse hard, so I moved to the edge of the narrow track to give them room to pass. I shook out my arms and used the excuse to take a break and enjoy the sun.

A massive black horse rounded the far bend at a full gallop. And perched atop it was a knight in shining silver chain mail with a huge broadsword strapped to his back. My lip curled, and it was an effort to smooth a pleasant look onto my face. Knights were *the worst*. High-handed and single-minded, they would rather stay doggedly obedient to their rotten king than listen to reason.

This one was handsome enough, as they often were, with short brown hair, dark eyes, and fair skin tanned from days in the sun. And not two brain cells to rub together, no doubt.

He reined in his horse as he neared, and my thoughts of a

warm fire and cozy books began to wane. I didn't have any desire to deal with a knight today.

The horse's lungs bellowed, and the poor creature was lathered in sweat. It shied as it neared, even though I stayed perfectly still.

The knight swung down from the saddle, but rather than ignoring his steed, he loosened the girth, took a cloth from his saddlebag, and started rubbing the horse down. "A moment, my lady," he said as he worked. "After I care for Percy, I will speak with you, if you'll allow it."

My eyebrows rose, both at his polite greeting and his concern for his horse. Perhaps I'd judged him too soon, because Percy was a whimsical name for a warhorse. Most were named *Killer* or *Vengeance* or *Thunder* or something equally ridiculous.

The knight caught my look and gave me a slightly embarrassed grin. "My sister breeds warhorses, and my young nephew picked this one for me—along with the name."

"It's lovely."

His smile grew, and he ducked his head. He couldn't have been more than twenty-five, as young and fresh as green spring leaves.

Once he finished wiping away the worst of the sweat, the knight led Percy in wide circles to cool down. I sipped from my canteen while I waited to see what he wanted. Both man and horse moved with the lithe grace of natural athletes. The horse didn't surprise me, but the man *did*. Knights were often overfed and overconfident, relying on reputation and brute strength rather than skill. If it came to a fight, he would be more dangerous than most.

Once the horse was cool, the knight returned and bowed. "I am Sir Ansel, at your service."

This close, I could see that his eyes were a dark brown, the warm color of rich soil. His hair was several shades lighter and clipped close to his head. He had a square jaw and a strong nose that were softened by a mouth that seemed to constantly smile. He was even more handsome up close.

I blinked and mentally shook my head, then responded a beat too late. "Feora."

"Lady Feora—"

"Just Feora," I interrupted.

He grinned at me, undaunted. "Just Feora, the road is too dangerous to travel alone. There was a dragon attack here less than two weeks ago. Please allow me to accompany you to your next destination."

"How many people did the dragon kill?"

Ansel blinked at me. "None that I am aware of, but a carriage full of the king's gold was stolen."

"Then I hardly have to worry, since I don't have a carriage full of gold."

"There are other concerns besides dragons, my lad—Feora. Bandits have been sighted in the nearby hills."

"On a dragon-blessed road?" I asked in disbelief. Surely no bandit would be so bold.

"I don't know about blessed," he said. "After the dragon steals its treasure, it moves on. The bandits can operate for weeks or months before they have to worry about another attack."

I hummed an acknowledgment as my thoughts whirled.

"The king has tasked me with hunting the dragon, but until the next sighting, I'm hunting bandits."

I waved at the road ahead. "Go on, then. Clear the way."

"You are a more tempting target than a knight, I'm afraid. I can't ensure your safety if I'm not with you."

I pointed at the sword hilt sticking out of my cart. "I can take care of myself."

"They'll take away my knighthood if I let a beautiful woman venture into dangerous woods alone," he said with a teasing smile. "Please reconsider."

I snorted at the flattery. My looks were perfectly average. My hair fell in dark waves past my shoulders, my eyes were just as dark, and my face was neither beautiful nor ugly. My most notable feature was my delicate-looking build, but I would disappear in a village of any size at all, overshadowed by the true beauties—and that was exactly how I liked it.

"No, thank you," I said, then gestured down the road. "Off you go."

He bowed. "As my lady commands."

CHAPTER 2

The dratted knight was once again waiting at the next bend in the road. For the past two hours, he'd ridden ahead as directed, but only as far as he could see me, or very slightly farther. Then he waited for me to approach before riding forward once more. He hadn't said a single word to me, hadn't even lifted an arm in greeting, but he was escorting me nonetheless.

It was two parts infuriating and one part intriguing.

"Wait," I called as he turned to continue. "If you're going to keep this up, you might as well ride with me."

His smile rivaled the sun, and my stomach did a weird little flip that I'd never felt before. Maybe the food at the last tavern hadn't agreed with me.

"Are you heading to Slyphon?" he asked.

I hadn't been, but I guess I was now, so I nodded.

He gave my cart a dubious glance. "It's three days on foot. Do you have sufficient supplies?"

He couldn't know the crates in my cart held only books, so I lifted my chin. "Of course. Do *you*?"

He patted the various saddlebags and bundles strapped to Percy. "I always carry extras, just in case."

Then the exasperating man dismounted and tried to hand me the reins, even as Percy danced sideways. "I will pull your cart while you take a break," he offered. "Do you know how to ride?"

"No, and I don't need a break." Belatedly, I remembered my manners and tacked on, "Thank you."

Now that I'd let him join me, he refused to ride while I walked, no matter how much I insisted I was fine and his armor was heavy. He wouldn't budge, so we started forward again side by side, accompanied by a soft symphony of clinking armor, shod hooves, and creaking wheels.

But it wasn't long before Ansel was regaling me with stories of his travels. His voice was smooth and soothing, like the best kind of tea. He was a natural storyteller, and his stories were funny and self-deprecating more often than not. The hours slid past, until the sun began to sink behind the trees.

"There's a stream up ahead," the knight said. "We can make camp nearby."

I shivered as the wind cut through my clothes. I hadn't planned to stay out past sunset, and certainly not with a knight. Once he fell asleep, I would slip away.

Ansel led me to a small clearing that had the look of a frequent travel stop. A ring of stones served as a fire pit, and a small pile of chopped wood waited nearby.

After a subtle glance at me, the knight dropped Percy's reins and started collecting kindling. The warhorse waited patiently, nibbling on the grass at his feet, while Ansel quickly built a fire.

I moved toward the stone ring as soon as the flames leapt toward the sky. Blessed warmth sank into my outstretched fingers.

Ansel turned to unsaddle his horse, and I crept closer to the fire. A moment later, warm, heavy material settled over my back and shoulders. I glanced up at the knight in surprise and started to shrug it away, but his big hands pulled the cloak together in front of me, cocooning me in warmth.

"As I said, I carry extras," he murmured. "Keep it. Please."

I swallowed and nodded, and he graced me with another radiant smile that made my stomach tremble.

He turned back to his things, rummaging around until he found a pot. He held it aloft like a prize. "I'll go fetch water and let Percy drink his fill. Shout if you need me."

I nodded again, and the knight and warhorse disappeared into the trees. The stream wasn't far, but I would be difficult to track in the growing darkness. Now would be the perfect time to leave, but the fire was warm, and I was strangely reluctant.

Ansel had been gone for less than five minutes when the first bandit slithered from the cover on the opposite side of the clearing, a drawn bow in his hands. His lips twisted into a mockery of a smile. "Stay quiet and we won't hurt you," he lied. "We just want the cart."

"You dare attack travelers on a dragon-blessed road?"

The bandit laughed and waved an arm toward the sky. "Do you see a dragon here?"

My smile turned sharp. "Come and take it, then, if you think you can."

Rather than wondering why a waif of a woman was taunting him, the bandit moved closer, five more rough-looking men on his heels. I flexed my hands under the cover of my cloak as my instincts awoke.

They were trying to take my books.

My treasure.

Mine.

The leader stopped in front of me, his face awash with covetous desire. The first swipe of my claws destroyed his bow, and the second destroyed his throat. He fell to the ground, dead before he knew he was under attack.

The others barely had time for surprise before they, too, met their ends.

I turned to take my cart and flee but paused at a distant shout and the sound of ringing swords.

The knight was fighting.

I told myself that it wasn't my battle, but the memory of his smile as he'd given me the cloak proved the words a lie.

I grabbed my sword and headed for the creek with a hissed curse.

WHEN I ARRIVED, the knight was outnumbered four to one, and the bandits were not fighting fair. Ansel was still standing, thanks to his armor and his sword's longer reach, but he'd taken damage. The two bodies on the ground proved he'd dealt some, too.

The first bandit didn't even notice me until my sword ran him through.

Ansel's eyes widened in alarm, and I wondered how I must look.

"Feora, run!" he shouted, and it was so surprising that I actually took a step back before remembering that *they* should run from *me*.

I roared a battle cry and launched myself at the next bandit. I batted his sword aside and swung for his neck. He did not survive.

Ansel used the distraction to kill one of the remaining bandits. The other took a wild swing at me. Ansel shouted a warning, but I blocked the blow with my arm.

Rather than biting in, the sword bounced away, ringing as if it had struck stone. The bandit paled, and my smile grew. He turned to run, but he died before he took the first step.

When it was just the two of us, Ansel didn't lower his sword, and sadness filled me. I didn't want this knight's life to end tonight.

"We don't have to fight," I murmured. "I have no quarrel with you."

He planted his sword in the ground a moment before he collapsed to one knee. Blood painted his lips, his wounds worse than I'd thought. "Lady Dragon," he whispered.

Then he fell face first into the dirt.

CHAPTER 3

Even in my dragon form, it took too long to gently carry Ansel back to my home. His breathing was shallow and reedy by the time I landed. But here, surrounded by my hoard, my magic was strongest.

And I refused to let the knight die tonight.

Even so, it took hours to stabilize him, and I was wan and weary by the time I was done. And I still needed to retrieve my books and Percy.

How I was going to manage to coax the horse within reach remained to be seen.

The books were easiest, so I retrieved them first. The cart was specifically designed to be carried by clawed feet, so it was a moment's work to add Ansel's things, then transform and grab it.

The horse was another matter. It shied every time I approached, even in human form. Fed up, I used a bit of my remaining magic to spell the beast asleep, then carefully picked it up and carried it home. I'd never needed the ancient stable attached to the courtyard, but it was useful now, if only to contain the horse until Ansel awoke.

Neither man nor beast would be able to leave the castle grounds without my permission.

I built a roaring fire in my bedroom fireplace, then curled up on the rug directly in front of it to soak up the warmth.

I was asleep as soon as I closed my eyes.

I AWOKE to the nearly silent sound of my bedroom door opening. The knight staggered inside, his footsteps unsteady. He really shouldn't be up yet, but I suppose my death was more important that his life.

Once again, sadness filled me.

A dagger left its sheath with a quiet hiss, and then he knelt next to me, body radiating warmth. I kept my eyes closed and my breathing deep and even.

Metal kissed my neck, and the blade trembled.

"Would you truly let me kill you so easily, Lady Dragon?" Ansel whispered.

I opened my eyes and lifted my chin, exposing more of my neck. "I am not so easily defeated, no. But go ahead, if you must try."

He lifted the blade from my skin as if I'd burned him.

"Why did you save me?" he demanded.

I sat up and met his eyes. "You were kind to me."

"I can't leave. Nor see anything beyond the castle walls."

"I know. Once you are healed, I will take you to whichever town you prefer, but you will be blindfolded and asleep. I've had enough torches and pitchforks in my life. I won't risk them again."

Ansel swallowed. "I suppose now I know how you came across the king's gold," he said. "I've been chasing you for months. A beautiful woman who only wants books, and always pays with a royal mark. You've become nearly a legend in the larger merchant circles."

"Did you know what I was?"

He laughed, but it was a hollow sound. "No, not until the sword bounced from your flesh without leaving a mark. I never even suspected. I thought perhaps you'd found the dragon's hoard and would be able to lead me to its hiding place."

I scoffed. "No one steals from a dragon and lives."

"So if I steal from you, you'll kill me?"

"Yes," I agreed, but it sounded like a lie.

He stared at me for a long moment before sheathing his dagger. He tried to bow, but he was hindered by his wounds and his armor, which I hadn't removed. "Thank you for saving my life. I am in your debt."

"Don't die and I'll consider it paid. You shouldn't be moving so much. I don't have the magic to heal you again today."

He glanced at the fire, and the rug, and the unused bed. "Do you normally sleep here?"

"No." I should've left it there, but I couldn't resist the curiosity in his eyes. "My body regenerates energy more quickly when I'm warm."

He twisted with a wince, reaching for the straps of his armor. He slowly unbuckled them, then pulled the chain mail over his head with a groan. I stared. He knew I was a dragon, but he had stripped away his main layer of protection anyway.

Not that it would've been *much* protection, but he didn't know that.

"What are you doing?" I asked.

"Sleeping in armor isn't comfortable." He set the armor aside, then slowly climbed to his feet. But rather than leaving, he dragged a blanket from the bed and returned.

He lay on the edge of the rug, then pulled the blanket over his body and held it open toward me. "I am warmer than the air."

I blinked at him in disbelief. "You can't be serious."

"I am."

"But I'm *a dragon*. You know, a big, scary, fire-breathing beast? The very thing the king has you hunting?"

"Are you going to eat me if I stay here?"

My spine straightened in outrage. "Of course not."

He shrugged. "Good enough for me. You saved my life. I'm tired. You're tired. I'm warm. You need warmth. Seems easy enough, but I will leave if that's your preference."

I hesitantly lay next to him, not quite touching, but close enough to feel the heat of his body.

He wrapped the blanket over me and tugged me closer. When I stiffened, he paused. "Is this okay?"

I nodded, then added, "I'm hard to kill. If you plan to try it, you'd better be sure you can finish the job."

He huffed out a soft breath that feathered over the back of my neck. "Sleep, Lady Dragon. You're safe with me."

"It's Feora," I murmured.

A quiet snore was his only answer.

CHAPTER 4

The next morning, I slipped from under Ansel's arm without disturbing him. I put more wood on the fire, then crept from the room.

Percy snorted at my approach but stood his ground. The water troughs in the stables were spring-fed, so the warhorse had plenty of water, and a bucket of grain had appeared overnight.

The knight must've been up for quite a while before finding my bedroom.

I carried the crates of books inside. I would shelve them later, but for now, I needed the handcart. I gathered some money—not royal marks this time—and my cloak, then set off for the nearby village.

As far as the villagers knew, I was a hermit who lived deep in the woods. Most of them thought I was a hedge witch, but my money was good, and I was polite, so they overlooked my eccentricities.

They had no idea what I *really* was, and I planned to keep it that way.

I bought enough food for two weeks, plus grain and hay for

Percy. The stable master raised her eyebrows at the unusual request, but she sold me the feed anyway.

The knight would likely be healed enough to travel in another day or two, but I would give the leftovers to the families in the village who needed it most, so it wouldn't go to waste.

I returned to the castle with my cart full of supplies. The knight was waiting for me by the front gate.

He looked over my shoulder, then frowned. Even though the gate was open, he wouldn't be able to see anything beyond the castle's outer wall.

"Where were you?" he demanded. Then, "Let me pull that."

I waved him off. The cart was heavy, and it didn't have any sort of clockwork-assist, despite what I often told curious merchants.

"You should be resting," I murmured as I passed him.

"I've rested enough."

That made me pause. I turned and let my magic trace over him. He wasn't fully healed, but he was well on his way thanks to my power. He would be okay to travel, at least for a short trip.

I suppressed a sigh. I'd been looking forward to company, strange as it was, but I wouldn't keep him here when he wanted to go.

I pulled the cart back into motion. It would need to be stored under cover until I could deliver the extra food back to the villagers. "Which village would you prefer?"

"What?"

"Where would you like me to take you?"

He jerked in surprise. "You're kicking me out? But I'm not healed."

My brows drew together. "You just told me you'd rested enough."

"And I have," he agreed. "But that doesn't mean I'm ready to leave." The corner of his mouth pulled up into a grin. "After all, I haven't seen your library, yet."

He couldn't know that asking to see a dragon's hoard was intensely intimate, but my stomach fluttered anyway.

I stopped the cart next to the stable and batted Ansel's hands away when he tried to grab the bale of hay. "I'll get it. You recover."

He shook his head. "I'm not going to let a lady haul supplies while I stand here."

I sighed. He might know I was a dragon intellectually, but he didn't really know what that *meant.* I turned and heaved the cart into the air, holding it over my head with ease. Ansel's mouth dropped open in stunned surprise, and he took a half step back before catching himself.

I carefully set the cart down again so I wouldn't have to see the fear in his eyes.

"That's incredible," he breathed. "How strong *are* you?" My gaze snapped back to him, but he continued without waiting for an answer. "You lifted a wagon full of gold, so you're exceptionally strong in your dragon form. Are you as strong as a human? Wait, you can transform. Can I see you in dragon form? Are there more dragons? How many?"

I held up a hand to stop the deluge of questions. "You're… you're not afraid?" I asked.

He tilted his head, regarding me with a steady gaze. "Should I be?"

I lifted one shoulder. "Most humans are."

"But should *I* be?" he asked again, softly.

"No. Not unless you're going to attempt to kill me."

He stepped closer, a tiny, secret smile on his face. "Then I have no reason to fear."

CHAPTER 5

The knight was damnably likable. He'd cheerfully ignored my orders to rest and recover, though he had let me carry the heaviest supplies, mostly because I'd growled at him when he'd tried it. He'd frozen for a moment before grinning at me and holding up his hands in surrender.

Now he was cooking breakfast, moving around the kitchen like he'd lived here his entire life. He had not donned his armor this morning, so his fragile skin was protected by only a thin layer of cloth.

Cloth that clung to his body in a highly flustering manner.

He drew my gaze like a magnet, and I knew I would have to send him on his way soon. Already, my instincts were stirring. Dragons are both possessive and territorial, and there's a reason we spend much of our time alone.

Ansel interrupted my thoughts by setting a plate in front of me with a flourish. "Your breakfast, my lady."

He'd made eggs, bacon, and crispy potatoes, along with a thick slice of toasted bread slathered in butter. My mouth watered. "Thank you."

He filled his own plate, then joined me at the table. We ate in silence for a while, then he asked, "What is your plan for the day?"

"The weather should be nice, so I need to spend some time in the garden." The warm sun would help the last of my magic recharge. "After that, I'll shelve my new books. I should probably also go patrol. I had no idea the bandits had gotten so bold lately. I need to teach them the error of their ways."

Ansel's eyes widened in understanding. "*You're* the reason people consider the roads dragon-blessed."

"The ones in my territory, yes. But I haven't been diligent enough. When you're as old as I am, time tends to pass differently."

"How old are you?"

The weight of my many years pressed on me. "Ancient."

He grinned before he realized I was serious. He shook his head in disbelief. "You don't look any older than me, and I'm twenty-nine."

He was older than I'd expected, but not by much. The weight of my years grew heavier. "I was ancient before you were born, and I'll be even more ancient after you are gone."

Something in my chest twisted at the thought of him old and gray and *dead*. He would be gone in a blink.

Unless…

I shut down that line of thought before it could form. I was perfectly happy alone and had been for the many long years of my life. I'd raised three broods—on my own, as is the way of dragons—before sending them out into the world to seek their fortune.

I did not want or need a mate.

No matter how pretty his brown eyes and muscled body.

I SHOWED Ansel how to weed the garden, and we worked in companionable silence. Well, *he* worked. I mostly lazed in the sun, basking in the warmth.

A shadow fell over me, and I cracked one eye open to find the knight grinning down at me, his brown hair haloed with sunlight like a golden crown. "I've done my half. Should I start on yours?"

"You should be resting. The weeds can wait."

"I'll rest if you show me your dragon form," he coaxed.

"You know I'm even harder to kill in that form, right?"

His brows drew together. "Why do you think I want to kill you?"

"You told me you were hunting the dragon who stole the king's gold. I am said dragon. Therefore, you are hunting me." I waved a hand at him. "It's what knights *do*."

He caught my fingers. His skin was warm under mine. "Perhaps, but not *this* knight. You are safe with me, Lady Dragon. I swear it, on my honor."

I studied him carefully. "You mean that, don't you?" He nodded, and I asked, "Why?"

"You are not a mindless killing machine. Neither am I."

When I stared at him in astonishment, he grinned and pulled me to my feet. "I'm feeling a desperate urge to weed your half of the garden, so if you want me to rest, you know what you have to do."

"Unfair," I grumbled, but I led him to the courtyard, where I'd have plenty of room to change. I backed him against the wall. His eyes lit with heated interest, and my stomach swooped.

I swayed toward him, my eyes locked on his lips, and his breath caught. He tipped his head down and reached for me with a groan. A heartbeat before our lips made contact, I remembered why kissing him would be a terrible idea.

I forced myself back a step, then pointed an unsteady finger at him. "Stay there. If it's too much, tell me and I will turn back."

He stared at me for a long moment, his eyes blazing, then he swallowed and dipped his head in agreement. Stepping away from him was surprisingly difficult. This was not good. He needed to leave, and soon.

I moved to the center of the courtyard. Changing forms was as easy as breathing. Magic rushed over my skin, and I let myself sink into my dragon form. My body expanded, sheathed in scales so deeply purple they were nearly black. Two legs became four, and wings sprouted from my back. My tail flicked through the air as the sun warmed me.

With sufficient sunlight, I could fly for a week without rest, even though my body was big and heavy. I was larger than the armored carriages I stole from the king, and I could look over the outer wall without stretching my neck—which is why the enchantment that hid the castle was anchored to the top of the keep.

I was delicate in my human form, but none of that delicacy remained in my dragon form. In this form, I was built for war and battle and death.

I stretched my wings wide, shading the entire courtyard, and I rumbled in contentment as the tough, leathery skin heated in the sun.

Ansel gasped.

I'd nearly forgotten about the knight, but a glance proved he'd stayed frozen in place. His mouth was slightly open, but it was awe on his face, not fear.

He looked up and met my gaze. "May I touch you?"

I rumbled my assent and settled onto the courtyard's warm stone pavers. I couldn't speak human language in this form, but the knight understood anyway.

He approached slowly, like I was a spooked animal, and his touch, when it came, was gentle. After a moment, he chuckled and tapped a knuckle against my scales. "No wonder you're hard to kill. I'm glad." He glided a hand down my side. "Can you feel that?"

I rumbled again, and he laughed in delight. "And I could feel *that*." He leaned his whole body against mine. "You're so warm. Is it the sun or your magic?"

It was both, so I gave him the same rumbling growl, and carefully wrapped my wing over him, cocooning him in warmth.

He yawned widely before shaking his head. "Now who's being unfair? You're going to make me so warm and comfortable that I'll fall asleep, and I still have a garden to weed."

I tucked him closer and crooned low in my throat. The part of me that had been clenched tight since he'd first gotten hurt finally relaxed. He was here. He was safe.

For now, it was enough.

CHAPTER 6

I awoke in human form with Ansel curled around me, his cloak over us both. The sun was still warm on my face, so we hadn't slept for more than an hour or two. I lingered, enjoying the warmth.

"You snore as a dragon *and* a human," the knight murmured, a smile in his voice.

"I should've eaten you when I had the chance," I grumbled without opening my eyes.

He chuckled, completely fearless. "Then who would pull the rest of the weeds, hmm? You'd better keep me around."

I sighed at the reminder. "You can't stay, Ansel."

He tensed beside me. "Why not?"

"It's not safe."

"You're a dragon, and I'm a knight. Surely we can—"

"It's not safe *for you*. My magic will enchant you whether I will it or not. It's already started. Would you have lain in the sun with a dragon a week ago?"

"I didn't know *you* a week ago," he argued, but I heard the tiny hesitation, the doubt.

Pain stole my breath. I didn't want to give him up, but I would. My fists clenched. *I would.* But first, I would show him the library.

I rose, then pulled him to his feet. "Come on."

He looked alarmed. "Are you kicking me out right this second?" I shook my head, and he sighed in relief. "Good."

I led him into the castle, and opened the magical locks on the library door. Then I pulled the key from thin air and turned the physical lock. The wide double doors swung open with a whisper of magic, revealing a vast room.

Ansel sucked in a surprised breath. The former gathering hall was enormous, and it was filled with bookshelves crammed with too many books. Most shelves were stacked two or three rows deep, and the balcony ringing the room held crates full of books that had nowhere else to live.

The knight looked at me with wide eyes. "Have you read all of these?"

"Yes, many times. Books help pass the time." He turned back to the room with a frown, no doubt mentally calculating how long that would take. I grimaced. "I told you I was ancient."

He smiled and shook his head. "I can't believe you use the king's gold to buy books. He's *furious* about the thefts."

"Good. I've gotten along with every previous monarch who has sat on the throne. But King Ordella discontinued the tribute payments, paltry though they were, and ordered his knights to hunt me. The gold is a reminder that I could do so much worse."

Ansel tilted his head. "Why don't you?"

"It's not my fight. Humans must decide their own fate. If the people rise up, I will aid them, as I always have. Until then, I do what I can."

The knight nodded thoughtfully, then delved deeper into the room. He ran his fingers along the book spines on the nearest shelf, and I shivered. Magic tightly bound me to my hoard. I would survive a total loss, but my power would be greatly diminished and my sorrow would be immense.

A hoard could be anything a dragon loved. Many coveted gold, jewels, and other shiny things. My distant cousin in the far north collected interesting rocks. Some—those who had lost their way—attempted to collect people.

Dragons rarely worked together, but eliminating the fallen among us was one instance where aid would be offered without reservation.

Ansel pulled a book from the shelf, and my magic pinged a warning.

He held the thin volume aloft. "So if I take this, you'll know?"

"Yes, and assuming you actually made it out of the castle alive, I could track it anywhere in the world."

He put the book back and looked around. "Do you have a favorite?"

"I have many favorites," I answered with a laugh. "What are you looking for?"

WE SPENT the rest of the afternoon in the library, and by the time we were done, the knight had a huge stack of books to read. I didn't have the heart to tell him that he wouldn't have enough time to read even one of them.

I helped him carry the books to his room, though it made my skin itch to have them outside the library.

He stopped me when I turned to leave. "Are you okay?" I nodded, and he drew me closer. "Are you sure?"

I wasn't, but I smiled anyway. "Yes. How are *you*?"

His expression turned guarded. "Still healing."

I didn't need to be a dragon to hear the lie, but I didn't call him on it. "In that case, I'll cook dinner."

"You can cook?" he asked in surprise.

My eyebrows lifted. "You think I eat peasants raw?"

He blinked, then a gorgeous smile broke across his face. His gaze settled on my lips, and he lifted a hand to my jaw, his touch featherlight.

I knew I should step away, but I couldn't quite convince my body to move.

I closed my eyes and leaned into the warmth of his fingers, promising myself that it would just be for a moment. How long had it been since I'd been this close to someone?

Dragons are solitary creatures. Offspring were usually produced via brief liaisons with temporary partners, and while broodlings sometimes remained in contact, other types of familial bonds were rare.

Few dragons ever found a life mate because few ever bothered to look for a compatible partner. But right now, my instincts were urging me to sink my claws into Ansel and keep him forever. I didn't want him as part of my hoard, I wanted *him*—whole and happy and *mine*.

He had to leave, tonight.

As if to test my resolve, Ansel brushed a soft, lingering kiss across my lips. I fought for control—*and lost.*

I clutched his shoulders and rose on my toes, deepening the pressure. He groaned and his mouth slanted over mine, intense and demanding.

I opened with a growl, and he licked my lip before tasting me. Desire roared through my blood, and I kissed him like his mouth held the secret to life. His arms wound around me, pulling me up against the hard warmth of his chest.

I groaned and maneuvered him backward until he sprawled across the bed, disheveled and glassy-eyed. I followed him down, straddling him and feeling exactly how much he wanted me. I rolled my hips and he grunted, then his hands clamped around my waist and pulled me snug against him.

The next slow grind felt even better.

Pleasure devastated me, and my fingers curled inward, a breath away from shredding his tunic. I wanted his skin against mine. I wanted to bask in his warmth. I *wanted…*

I shook my head and fought to remember why I couldn't have him. "Tell me no," I demanded.

His smile was warm and wicked. "I'm telling you *yes.*"

A pleased, possessive growl rumbled out of me before I could stop it. My fingers flexed and the sound of ripping fabric was just enough to break the haze of pleasure.

I leapt back, landing in a crouch on the floor. "Did I hurt you?"

Ansel blinked, then sat up and frowned at me. "No. You didn't even touch my skin." He lifted a hand. "Come back."

The soft invitation was nearly enough to break my will.

I pulled myself together with iron discipline, then stood on shaky legs. "You are not safe here. You need to leave. Where do you want to go?"

His eyes widened. "Feora, no," he pleaded. He stood and closed the distance between us. "This isn't because of your magic. It's *you.* I want to stay. You must believe me."

I pressed my finger to his lips before he could shatter me completely. "The magic will fade in a week or two, and you'll look back at this time and wonder what you were thinking."

He pulled my fingers away from his mouth, but didn't let go of my hand. "I won't," he disagreed, his voice hard.

"You will."

His eyes narrowed. "I won't leave."

I lifted our entwined fingers, brushed a kiss across his knuckles, and repeated, "You will."

"At least give me time to pack my things and tend to Percy."

Every second was like a lethal dagger in my heart, but I nodded my agreement. "I will await you in the courtyard. Don't tarry."

I fled the room before I could change my mind, but not even the library could soothe my turmoil. I'd had liaisons with humans before, and none had affected me so. I would think the knight had enchanted *me* if I wasn't immune to magic.

I took a deep breath and tucked my emotions away. There would be time to mourn later. Now I had a knight to free.

CHAPTER 7

Ansel was waiting for me in the courtyard, Percy at his side. The knight's jaw was clenched, and his expression blazed with stubborn determination.

"I'll find you," he declared. "No matter how long it takes."

"People have been looking for me for hundreds of years. None have succeeded."

"They weren't me," he said with the boundless arrogance I usually associated with knights. Finally, he was starting to act his part, but it was too late.

I'd already fallen.

"They weren't you," I agreed softly. "But in a few weeks, this will seem like nothing more than a strange dream."

His eyes narrowed. "We shall see."

"Are you ready?"

He took three long strides, then his arm clamped around me like an iron band. He tilted my head back and glared at me. "Next time I find you, you won't send me away. Swear it."

I silently shook my head.

"Swear it, and I'll leave without another protest." His expression hardened. "Or don't, and I will fight you the entire time."

I closed my eyes. If he fought, I wasn't sure I was strong enough to let him go. "Very well, if you find me again, and it's at least two months from now, I will not send you away. I swear it."

A muscle in his jaw flexed at the additional clause, but he nodded his agreement. Then his mouth was on mine, a hot, hard kiss that felt like a brand.

He jerked back, leaving me shaky and off balance. "I'm ready," he growled.

∼

I GENTLY LAID Ansel on the pallet of blankets I'd made in the soft grass. He was frowning even in sleep, but this was for the best. He would realize that as soon as my magic faded.

Percy was tied nearby, and the warhorse watched me with a wary eye. He'd stopped shying every time I approached, but I'd still put him to sleep for the trip. Even the bravest horses didn't enjoy being picked up and hauled through the air by a massive predator.

The rest of Ansel's gear was neatly piled next to him. I checked it again, though I already knew everything was there. I was lingering unnecessarily, but I couldn't quite make myself stop.

After a long moment, I knelt and pulled the pilfered book from the knight's pocket with a bittersweet smile. I'd known the moment he'd taken it, of course. He had bravery to spare, because I'd warned him I would kill anyone who stole from me.

But I'd also told him I could track the book anywhere in the world.

He wanted me to find him, consequences be damned.

I pulled out the note I'd hastily scrawled while in the library. It was short, just a single line: *Forget me, and be happy.*

I tucked the paper into his pocket with a handful of silver, then kissed his forehead. I curled my fingers against the urge to grab him and spirit him back to my castle as fast as I could fly.

I had to let him go. I closed my eyes. I *had* to.

Every instinct screamed in vicious denial.

I forced myself to my feet, then strode into the trees to watch over him until he awoke, all while pretending I felt nothing at all.

CHAPTER 8

Six months later…

The weather was cold and gray, and if not for persistent rumors of bandits along this road, I would've been tucked into my cozy castle with a book and a roaring fire. I'd still be miserable, but at least I'd be *warm* and miserable.

This was my second attempt to flush the bandits out, but I'd yet to see any sign of them. Either they were smarter than usual or they'd moved on, and the rumors hadn't caught up.

By the time the next town came into view, I was frozen and surly. The smart choice would've been to return to my castle, but for the past six months my home had been unbearably lonely.

The knight hadn't found me—and hadn't even looked, as far as I could tell. A month after I'd let him go, I'd started lingering in towns across the area, hoping for even a hint of rumor about a knight searching for a dragon, but there hadn't been a single whisper. It was just as I'd expected. My heart ached, but I'd gotten used to ignoring it.

I trudged toward the nearest tavern. I would warm up with a

hot meal and listen for any new bandit rumors, then I would return home and brood in peace.

I was so busy ignoring everything that I nearly missed the sign. Even after it registered, I blinked twice, sure I was hallucinating.

My eyes traced over the freshly carved and painted wood, drinking in every detail. Raised white text spelled out "Books & Broadswords" over a background of dark dragon scales. The logo was a coat of arms with two broadswords crossed behind an open book.

It was, in a word, *perfect*.

The shop's windows blazed with light, and a peek through the glass proved that half of the shelves were indeed packed with books while the other half were filled with weapons and armor. For the first time in months, I felt the familiar prickle of avarice.

This shop had not been here on my last visit.

Not only that, but it seemed designed specifically for me. If it was a trap, it was a clever one. If not…

I wavered, aware exactly who might be lurking inside. Hope demanded action, but honor held me back. I could walk away now, and he would never know. But I would never know, either.

Was the knight waiting inside, or would a stranger call out a greeting and break my heart?

The door opened before I could decide. Ansel stepped out into the cold evening air, looking even more handsome than I remembered. He wore a tunic and trousers, no armor in sight.

He slanted an unreadable glance at me. "I told you I would find you."

"If we're being technical, *I* found *you*," I said around the sudden lump in my throat.

His brow furrowed into a scowl. "Who do you think has been spreading rumors of bandits for months?" He scoffed. "Took you long enough."

I wasn't sure what to do with this prickly version of the

knight who'd once smiled at me with utter delight, but my instincts were screaming at me to snatch him up before he escaped again.

I clasped my hands together under my cloak until my fingers ached. "Is this your store?"

"If we're being technical," he drawled, echoing my earlier words, "it's *yours*."

"What do you mean?"

"Your gold paid for it. Well, originally, it was the king's gold, I suppose, but I stole it from you." He tilted his head. "You didn't notice?"

"No." Gold wasn't part of my hoard, so it wasn't tied to me with magic. It was useful, but that was it.

"You noticed the book." His voice was soft.

"From the moment you took it," I agreed.

He slanted another glance at me. "You didn't kill me."

I swallowed. "No. But I couldn't let you keep it, either. The temptation would've been too much."

He regarded me steadily. "For you or me?"

"For me," I whispered. "If I'd known where you were, I never could've let you go."

"I told you I didn't want to leave."

"You were enchanted. I *had* to let you go."

"I wasn't, and you didn't," he said. "It's been six months and my feelings haven't changed."

I squinted at him. I'd never heard of an enchantment lasting that long, but perhaps I'd dosed him with more of my magic than I'd realized.

He chuckled, but the sound had a bitter undertone that grated against my ears. "You still think I don't know my own heart," he murmured, shaking his head.

He turned and backed me against the window, his eyes blazing, and his body a wall of heat. "Let's get one thing straight, Lady Dragon," he growled. "I knew you were it for me from your very first scowl. So unless your magic works instantaneously, I was not magically enchanted."

"But I'm a dragon."

"That was a bit of a surprise," he agreed with the shadow of a grin. "But now that I've found you again, I'm not letting you go. Would you like to see your new books?"

I closed my eyes against the temptation. "Unfair," I murmured.

His lips skimmed over my jaw. "Oh, Feora, I haven't even started."

CHAPTER 9

The store looked like it had been pulled directly from my imagination. A roaring fire kept the room toasty, and comfortable chairs were scattered around the walls. Half of the space was filled with rows of bookshelves laden with books, including many foreign volumes I'd never been able to get my hands on.

My fingers itched. I hadn't brought any gold, since I hadn't expected to be shopping today, so I made note of the books I wanted most. The list grew so large that it became easier to keep track of the books I already had.

Ansel watched me without comment.

It was fully dark by the time I ventured into the other half of the store. It was filled with weapons and armor of the highest caliber. I lifted a perfectly balanced short sword and smiled at the delicate craftsmanship. I would add this to my purchase, too.

Ansel's broadsword hung behind the counter, along with his chain mail. I frowned, and he spoke for the first time in hours. "I gave up my knighthood."

"Why?"

He waved an arm at the room. "I decided to start dragon

hunting on my own. But I was beginning to think I'd have to take up banditry before you'd notice me."

"You built this store for me." It was both a statement and a question.

He smiled softly. "Yes, but it turns out that the concept is surprisingly popular. Knights come in for the weapons and armor, but they leave with books, too."

He saw my grimace and grinned. "I have duplicates of every book on the shelves. Your future hoard is safe."

My eyes widened. "Just how much gold did you steal?"

"A *lot*. I expected you to hunt me down for it. When you didn't, I figured I would have to take drastic measures."

"I didn't leave my castle for a month," I admitted.

He slowly closed the distance between us. "Why?"

"Because I would've found you and dragged you back. I locked myself in the library and reorganized the entire collection for the first time in a hundred years. Now I can't find anything." When his smile grew, I glared at him. "It's not funny."

He drew me close. "I'll help you put it back. I've learned a bit about shelving books."

I leaned against his chest. "You have to be sure," I whispered. "Really, really sure. Because dragons are possessive, and I'm no exception. I don't know if I'll be strong enough to let you go again."

"Well, it turns out, former knights are possessive, too. And I'm sure. Really, really sure. Would you like to see your private library upstairs?"

I froze and leaned back enough to see his face. "You built me a library?"

"I told you I wasn't planning to play fair. The bedroom has two fireplaces—but only one bed. How do you feel about sharing?"

He was still smiling, but I could see the uncertainty in his eyes. I lifted onto my toes and brushed a delicate kiss over his lips. "In this case—and this case only—I'd love to share."

Heat slowly burned away his uncertainty, and he blew out a deep breath before nuzzling my temple like he couldn't believe I was really here. "I missed you."

"I've been miserable without you," I admitted.

He lifted me up to sit on the counter, then wedged himself between my thighs. "You should've listened to me, Lady Dragon."

I reached for him and the hard muscles of his abdomen twitched under my fingers. "I'm sorry I hurt you." I met his eyes, so he would see the truth of that statement.

After his chin dipped in acknowledgment, I let my smile grow playful. "Perhaps I can begin to make amends if you show me this one bed you're so proud of?"

His smile matched mine. He pressed a swift, hard kiss to my lips before scooping me off the counter with ease. "Deal."

∾

THE NEXT MORNING, Ansel padded into the library wearing a low-slung pair of trousers and nothing else. The room was delightfully warm, even with the bitter wind outside, and I rumbled in contentment.

The former knight leaned against the nearest shelf and crossed his arms, silently showing off his physique. When my growl deepened, he grinned at me. "You're the one who left the bed, not me."

"You can't build me a library and then expect me not to spend time in it."

He leaned down and pressed a kiss to my lips. "Spend as much time as you like. Do you want to move the books to your castle?"

The question was casual, but there was something in his tone that pulled my attention away from the book in my hand. I frowned at him. "Do you want me to?"

"I mapped every dragon attack for the last hundred years," he said instead of answering. "This was the center. How close is your castle?"

I tilted my head in thought. "Maybe an hour by horse."

He blinked. "So far?"

"Yes. Putting my castle dead center in my territory would make it a target. You're not the first to use the attacks to try to find me. But I can make the same trip in ten minutes in my dragon form."

"Why don't the surrounding villagers know where you live?"

"Magic, mostly. Dragons can move unseen." I met his eyes. "Why don't you want me to move the books?"

He grimaced slightly and ran a hand through his hair. "It's not that," he said. "I built all of this for you. The books are yours. But over the last few months, I've actually come to enjoy running the shop. I like talking to people and being part of the community. My sister and nephew are half an hour away." He sighed. "I guess I'm worried that if you take the books, you won't have any reason to return."

I stood and gently turned his face back to mine. "I'll have *you*, Ansel. You'll always be more important than books. If you want to stay here, we can. I can add these books to my hoard without moving them." It would be a little more difficult, but it wasn't impossible. And the magic would strengthen the protections on the shop, too.

"What happens when I get old and gray and you tire of me?"

I kissed his jaw. "I will never tire of you. You're my mate, the match to my soul. If you are willing, I can tie your life to mine, and you will age like a dragon. If not, I'll cherish the time we have together—all of it."

"If I grow old and die, what will happen to you?"

Now it was my turn to glance away. "I would mourn." And

then I would die. Losing a life mate early wasn't fatal, but after a lifetime together, I wouldn't be able to continue alone. I wouldn't *want* to.

I turned back to him. "The mating is permanent, which is why you need to be very sure. Once you agree, we will be bound for eternity, or close enough."

A tender smile broke across his face. "Are you asking me to marry you? If so, the answer is yes."

I smiled and slightly shook my head. "I will happily marry you, but a mate bond is deeper than that. You need time to learn about the consequences before you decide. If you feel the same way in a year, we will move forward." Waiting a year would be excruciating, but I would find a way to do it.

Until then, I would guard him like the treasure he was.

EPILOGUE

I paced out my anxiety on top of the castle's keep. I did not need to look at the calendar to know the importance of today's date. It had been one year, six months, and ten days since I'd first met Ansel, and exactly one year since I'd offered to make him my mate.

Time might pass differently for dragons, but that didn't mean we couldn't track it precisely when the mood suited us.

Ansel had often pestered me in the early days to mate him immediately, but he hadn't mentioned it in months, and I secretly wondered if he'd changed his mind. I was bracing for rejection even as I hoped for acceptance.

The last year had been one of the happiest in my long life.

Our store was flourishing, and if the townsfolk had any suspicions about my true nature, they kept them to themselves, especially since the crime rate had dropped dramatically since I'd arrived.

Ansel's family was delightful, and they'd welcomed me with open arms.

I still stole the king's gold with clockwork regularity, but since Ansel bought me as many books as I could ever want, I melted the royal marks and recast them into dragon coins that I gave to those who needed help.

It infuriated the king, but after several of his knights had met untimely ends while trying to punish people for using the new coins, he'd grudgingly relented. Or perhaps it had been my visit to his castle in my dragon form. Either way, dragon marks were now considered legal tender, and many considered them lucky.

Even Percy had settled enough that I no longer spooked him, and he allowed me to ride with Ansel with only a snort or two of complaint.

The warhorse was grazing on my garden while the former knight worked on some project or other. I should be helping him, but it'd been all I could do to act natural through breakfast. I wouldn't pressure him, no matter how much I wanted to.

He would decide when he was ready, or he wouldn't, and I would respect his decision either way.

Even if it killed me, which it might.

I was a breath away from transforming and taking my nerves out on any hapless bandits I could find when I heard footsteps.

Ansel crested the stairs with a smile. "There you are. Enjoying the sun?"

I nodded, my heart in my throat. I didn't know how he became even more gorgeous every time I saw him, but I suspected it was magic.

He crossed the roof with a soft look on his face. "You think I forgot."

"Forgot what?" I tried, but my voice came out hoarse.

He lifted my hand and brushed a kiss across my knuckles. "You can't fool me, Lady Dragon. I know you too well." He slipped a golden band onto my ring finger. Books, broadswords, and dragon scales were delicately carved onto its surface. "I wanted to finish it before I asked," he whispered. "Sorry I kept you waiting."

I dragged my gaze away from the beautiful ring long enough

to meet his eyes, fragile hope blossoming in my chest. "Ask what?"

"Marry me, Feora. Mate me. Make me yours, forever. It's been a year. I understand what I'm asking, and my feelings haven't changed."

"You're sure?" I asked, even as magic roiled under my skin, desperate to bind him before he could change his mind.

His smile was brighter than the sun. "I'm sure. Make me yours."

I closed my eyes and fought for control. "Now?" I pleaded.

"Yes. What do I—"

The rest of his sentence was lost as my magic exploded from me and wrapped us together, binding us with unbreakable bonds. He was *mine*. I roared my claim to the heavens.

Ansel kissed me, and my heart settled. His lips were warm and firm even as magic continued to whirl around us. "Finally," he murmured against my skin.

I laughed in delight. I couldn't have said it better myself.

ROCKS & RAPIERS

CHAPTER I

Wading through shin-deep snow all morning had given me plenty of time to reconsider the wisdom of plans conceived in the dark, desperate hours before dawn. But I *was* desperate, so I trudged onward. This would work.

It *had* to work.

I was wearing two pairs of socks and fur-lined boots, but my toes were starting to go numb by the time the remote manor emerged from the trees. It was hard to pinpoint exactly why, but the dark stone facade felt unwelcoming in a way that made my instincts prickle. Only the brave—or foolish—would approach such a place.

Unfortunately for me, I was both.

I hitched my pack higher on my back and made my way to the entrance. A shiver that had nothing to do with the cold worked its way down my spine, but I hadn't come this far to turn back now.

My mitten-covered fist barely made a sound on the heavy door, so it didn't surprise me when no one answered. I knocked again, and again, and then I tried the handle.

The door opened.

"Hello!" I called through the crack. "Is anyone home? I've come to barter!"

Resounding silence answered me. I pushed the door open wider and tried again. "I'm just going to wait inside, if that's okay with you."

I stomped the snow from my boots and eased through the doorway. It felt wrong to enter someone's house without an invitation, but for all the place appeared abandoned, it was *warm*.

The door closed behind me with an ominous *thud*. I immediately tried the handle again and the door opened. I was not trapped. I let out a slow breath and tried to get my pulse to settle.

"What are you doing in my house?" a deep voice demanded from directly behind me.

I screeched as my heart leapt from my body. I twisted so quickly my pack overbalanced me, and I ended up on the floor, staring up at the most striking man I'd ever seen.

Tall and blond, he would've been handsome if his frosty stare hadn't been exactly as unwelcoming as the manor's facade. He stared down his straight nose at me, and did not look impressed at what he saw.

My shoulder-length brown hair was usually neat and straight, but the wind had tangled it into a snarl, and my clothes were well-worn and damp from the snow. My hazel eyes were unusual enough to garner a second glance, but this man could give icicles lessons on how to be cold and forbidding.

I huffed at him and climbed to my feet with as much dignity as I could muster—which wasn't much. "I'm here to barter," I repeated, unsure if he'd heard my initial shout.

"How did you find this place?"

"I followed the path."

At this, he frowned. "From the village?"

"Yes?" I hadn't meant to make it a question, but where else would I be coming from? "I've brought rocks to trade."

One pale eyebrow rose over his icy blue eyes. "Rocks?"

"Yes. I've heard you will trade for interesting rocks. I have a collection I've been gathering for years."

His expression gave nothing away. "From whom have you heard such?"

"You know… people," I hedged with a breezy wave. In point of fact, I'd heard a sketchy rumor several years ago, then the person I'd heard it from had disappeared without a trace, hopefully to their new life of fortune and not into a shallow grave.

I had a sword and the skill to wield it, so I wasn't *too* concerned. Though, looking at the man before me, perhaps I should've been. He was unarmed, but that didn't mean he wasn't dangerous. He was lean and muscular, and if he caught me, he'd easily overpower me.

"Show me what you brought," he said at last.

Relief nearly buckled my knees. I looked around the empty entryway, then promptly wished I hadn't as my instincts forcefully demanded I banish the dust and restore the room to cleanliness. The grime clinging to every surface rang like a discordant note, overpowering the house's lovely underlying chord.

I swallowed and pretended I couldn't see the neglect or hear the house's song, muted though it was. The entry was nice and warm, but there wasn't a single table to be found. I glanced at the man. "Don't you want to move to a sitting room or study or whatever kind of room a fancy house like this has? Preferably one with a table?"

And preferably one that's clean. I mentally crossed my fingers and hoped for the best.

The man gave me a long-suffering sigh, but he turned and started down the hall. "Follow me."

THE BLOND MAN led me deeper into the building. The hallway was as warm as the entryway but just as dusty. Cobwebs clung to the corners of the ceiling. Someone had made a half-hearted attempt to clean the floor, then tracked muddy foot-prints in.

My fingers itched with the need to set the house to rights, to smooth out the dissonant notes until the song was bright and clear, but I wasn't here to work.

"I'm Zenira," I said as a distraction.

The man continued walking in silence, as if he hadn't heard me, but I wasn't so easily dissuaded. "And you are?"

He slanted a dark glance at me over his shoulder. "Busy."

"Oh, I'm sorry. Am I keeping you from your important work of lording over the local peasants? Because I'm certainly not keeping you from cleaning."

The last part was mumbled, but he stopped and turned all the way around, a dangerous look on his face. "What did you say?"

I gestured at the fancy house surrounding us. "You *are* the lord of this county, aren't you? If so, you're doing a poor job—on multiple fronts, it seems." I squinted at him, reconsidering. "Or are you a smuggler?"

"I am neither, which you should be grateful for, assuming you actually planned to leave here alive." His eyes flicked down to the rapier hanging at my side. "Can you use that?"

Fear finally caught up to me, and I swallowed. "Yes. Am I going to need to?"

Rather than answering, he turned and opened the nearby door. "Your table, as requested."

He'd brought me to the dining room. A table big enough to seat ten filled the room, and its polished surface gleamed in the lamplight. Finally, one thing in this house was clean.

I shrugged off my pack, then reconsidered my plan to put it on the table. Who knew what the grouchy man looming behind me would do if I put so much as a single scratch on his fancy tabletop. Better to be safe.

As I set the pack on the floor, my stomach growled. I ignored it, but the man sighed. "Wait here. Do not leave this room until I return. Do you understand?"

Embarrassment heated my cheeks. "You don't have—"

The door clicked closed behind him. He moved far too quietly for such a tall man. Smuggler was starting to look more and more likely.

I draped my cloak over one end of the table, then laid out the rocks I'd brought. This was my entire collection, gathered over the course of my thirty-one years. Most of it was hardly worth mention, except for sentimental value, but I'd brought everything, hopeful that something in the hoard would catch his eye.

Maybe he would like the geode with the pretty purple crystal inside. Or the smooth white rock with the tiny fossil embossed on its surface.

Or maybe he would like none of it and this trip was a waste of time.

My stomach growled again, upset about the lack of lunch. I had a muffin in my pack, but I hadn't wanted to remove a mitten to eat it, so I'd ignored the hungry grumbles.

Once I'd arranged the collection into neat rows, I hovered awkwardly next to the table. I didn't dare sit on any of the delicately carved chairs. They looked like they'd collapse in a brisk breeze, and I couldn't afford to replace one.

The man returned a few minutes later, carrying a tray topped with a steaming bowl. He set the tray on the end of the table not covered by my cloak, and I tried not to look too hopeful. Perhaps he'd just gotten hungry and now expected me to watch him eat.

I dragged my eyes away from the bowl and ordered my stomach not to embarrass me further.

"Sit," the man said, pointing at the chair next to the tray. "I will examine your collection while you eat."

I eyed him warily. "What will the meal cost me?"

His spine stiffened, and the dangerous look returned. "You are a guest in my house, however unwanted. Do not insult my hospitality by presuming that I would demand payment for food."

"I meant no insult, but I've learned it's best to be clear." Especially with people in positions of power.

"Eat, Zenira. The meal is freely given, and I expect nothing in return."

I rounded the table and pulled out the chair, surprised that it was sturdier than it appeared. Still, I perched on the edge, unwilling to risk damaging it or staining the upholstered cushion.

The bowl was filled with a thick potato soup that smelled absolutely divine. I'd burned a lot of energy traipsing through the snow, and the soup was warm and filling.

While I ate, the man examined every rock, fossil, and crystal I'd brought with a thoroughness that told me he either knew *a lot* about rocks or nothing at all.

Or he was stalling for time.

The last was proved true when I carefully set my spoon next to the empty bowl, and he immediately said, "I will pay you ten silver for the lot."

"You want them all?" I asked, sure I'd heard incorrectly. I'd expected him to choose two or three of the best specimens, not all of them. Most of the rocks were far more sentimental that valuable, and parting with them would wound.

When his chin dipped in agreement, I swallowed. I needed the money, and they were only rocks. There were a thousand more just outside the door. But those weren't *mine*.

"Can I keep a few?" I whispered.

"The offer is for the whole lot. Take it or leave it."

I clenched my fingers together. Years of my life, gone in a heartbeat. But ten silver was more than I could make in three months, and it would be enough to keep me housed this winter.

Hopefully.

The local landowner had unexpectedly passed away two months ago, and now the distant relation who had inherited wanted to evict me and rent the house to a tenant who would bring in more money. I'd had a perpetual rental agreement that locked in my rent, but it wasn't in writing, so the new landowner refused to honor it.

He'd set the rent to what a tenant farmer with a successful harvest would pay. He knew I couldn't afford it, and he didn't care in the slightest.

Most of my neighbors were in similar straits, and everyone was scrambling to scrounge up enough money to keep a roof over their heads. Jobs were thin on the ground.

I touched the sparkly rock I'd picked up while on a walk with my mom. I'd been so sure that it was filled with gold or treasure, but it was just bits of quartz. Pretty, but worthless.

I refused to make the obvious comparison. I was not worthless, no matter what the landowner or the king and his knights thought.

I blinked back tears and nodded at the nameless man. "Ten silver. I agree."

The soft *clink* of coins on the table very nearly broke me, but I straightened my spine. This was why I'd come. I should be grateful that anyone even *wanted* rocks.

Life had stolen most of the other reminders of my mother, so why not this one, too? At least I'd gotten a meal out of it, and my toes were starting to thaw. My trip back would be faster without the extra weight in my pack, so I'd make it well before sunset.

It was fine. Everything was fine. The part of me that felt like it was laid bare and dying would just have to get over it. If I didn't have money for shelter this winter, then I would *literally* die.

The man gestured at the ten silver coins, neatly laid out for easy counting. I only hesitated for a moment before swiping them off the table with a nod. I partially unlaced my boot so I could get to the hidden pocket I'd added inside, and my toes throbbed.

Maybe not thawed after all.

I secured the silver then laced the boot tight. By the time I was done, my collection had disappeared. It felt like a dagger to the gut, but I kept the tears locked behind iron will.

My pack was featherlight as I swung it over my shoulder. The damp cloak went on next, and then I had no more reason to linger in the warmth. I dipped my head at the man who had given me another few months to live.

Maybe it would be enough.

CHAPTER 2

The manor door closed behind me with quiet finality. The wind sliced through my cloak with bitter teeth, but I couldn't afford a heavier one, even with the silver in my boot.

I followed my own footprints back toward the village. With every step, it was a struggle not to turn back. Leaving my collection behind was difficult enough, but leaving the manor in such a sorry state went against my every instinct. The discordant notes haunted me, begging me to smooth them away. Only the thought of the unnamed man's frosty expression kept me on the path.

My cottage was cold and dark by the time I made it home, and my fingers and toes were icy. I built a small fire in the stove with the last of my coal. Tomorrow, I would need to buy more.

This morning's gruel had congealed into a solid brick, but I put the pan on the stove and added a little water. I could go to the tavern for dinner, but I needed every piece of silver in my boot just to cover rent, and my savings were already depleted. I couldn't afford a solicitor to fight the landowner, so I'd be forced to move in the spring, which meant economizing everywhere I could.

I ate huddled in a blanket next to the stove. But for all my cottage was bare, it was *clean,* and its song was clear and happy. The manor's state lingered in the back of my mind, like a partially remembered thought or a half-finished job.

And no matter how many times I reminded myself that it wasn't my problem, I couldn't quite escape the desire to set it to rights.

I AWOKE the next morning tired and grumpy. I hadn't slept well at all, and something must be done about the manor's state, frostiness be damned. I shoved a week's worth of clothes into my pack and doubled up my socks for another long trudge through the snow.

First, I stopped at the landowner's secretary's office and paid my rent. The man accepted the payment with a pained grimace. He, too, lived in the village and had no doubt gotten an earful from all of his neighbors, but it wasn't his fault his new boss was a such an ass.

I sighed in resigned relief as I stepped outside. Now I had three months of breathing room to find a new place to live.

And a potential job just waiting for me to grab it.

The trip through the snowy forest wasn't any more pleasant, but as the manor finally came into view, I felt lighter. I pounded a fist on the door and waited.

And waited.

And waited.

I knocked again, and when that didn't result in the door opening, I tried the latch. It was unlocked, so I let myself in with a shrug. If the owner didn't want me inside, he should've locked his door after yesterday.

"Hello!" I called as the door closed behind me.

The man appeared at the top of the stairs, frosty glare firmly in place. "You again."

It wasn't exactly the most welcoming of greetings, but I forged ahead anyway. "Me again," I confirmed. "I'm here for a job."

"I don't recall posting any jobs."

"You need someone to clean your house, and I need money. Hire me as a maid for a week, and I'll make the floors gleam. I'll clean the entire house for twelve silver plus room and board."

His eyebrows rose. "Most maids make a single silver in a week, if that."

"I'm not most maids. If you'd like to hire a dozen others to do the work, you can. But *someone* needs to clean this house because it's a disgrace."

He descended the steps in silence, and I wondered if I was about to be tossed out into the snow. He stopped close enough that it would be difficult for me to draw my sword and took a deep breath.

Something like surprise crossed his face before he smoothed it away. "Very well. One week, twelve silver. But if you don't finish the entire house, I won't pay you the full amount."

"That's fine," I agreed before he could change his mind—or think to negotiate. "If you'll point the way to the staff quarters, I'll change and get started. How would you prefer to be addressed?"

"Baldric."

"Very well, Lord Baldric, thank you for this opportunity." I dropped into a passable curtsy.

"I'm not a lord," he said. Before I could correct myself, he asked, "Have you eaten lunch?"

My stomach remained blissfully silent. "Not yet."

He pointed up the stairs. "Choose any room on the second floor except the one at the end of the hall, then meet me in the kitchen."

I curtsied again, but Baldric was already turning away. I climbed the stairs to the second floor. It was only marginally cleaner than the floor below, and I winced. The thick carpet runners in the hallway desperately needed a good beating as well as a snow scrub. Luckily, we were in the season for it.

I wanted to stay as far as possible from the double doors at the end of the hall, so I opened the first door I came to. My breath caught. The bedroom walls were coated in pale peach plaster, and the delicate furniture was painted a complementary light green. The whole room reminded me of spring, and I couldn't believe Baldric was going to allow me to stay here for a week.

A fine layer of dust coated everything, the room's hum off-key and grating, so I set my pack on the floor and carefully changed into a gray working dress, white apron, and sturdy slippers. The rugs would have to wait until my toes thawed once more.

I tied my straight brown hair back with a white kerchief, then peered at myself in the dusty vanity mirror. I looked respectable enough now, but I would be coated in grime by the time I finished for the day.

I returned to the ground floor while mentally compiling a task list. I'd need to see the other levels before beginning, but if they were anything like what I'd already seen, I'd have my work cut out for me.

At least while Baldric was awake. Once he was safely abed, I could work faster.

Much faster.

I pushed the door open into a surprisingly clean kitchen filled with the delicious aroma of chicken soup. For the first time, the house's chord was unmarred, a deep lovely sound that made me smile.

Baldric sat at the end of the battered table with a steaming bowl in front of him. He'd placed another bowl—presumably for me—on his left, where my back would be to the wall.

I'd left my sword behind, but I had a small knife hidden in my apron's front pocket. I circled the far end of the table, then pulled out the stool and sat. "Is the cook not joining us?"

"I don't have a cook," he said.

No maids, no cook. In fact, as far as I could tell, he didn't have any household staff at all. What kind of person was wealthy enough to have this fancy house and spend silver on *rocks*, but didn't have staff?

Someone who didn't want anyone poking into his business, most likely.

I shook my head. It wasn't my concern. Once the house was clean, I'd be on my way. I pulled my bowl toward me. It was filled with a hearty chicken and noodle soup that had actual chunks of chicken in it. He'd also given me a cup of clear, cold water, along with a cup of tea.

"Thank you for the food," I murmured.

His eyebrows rose slightly. "If you're planning to clean this entire house in a week, you'll more than earn it."

I nodded in agreement. It was clear that he didn't expect me to finish the whole house, but if he kept feeding me like this, I might get done early.

We ate in silence. It wasn't entirely comfortable, but it also wasn't as awkward as I'd expected. I finished the last of my soup, then drained the final drops of tea from my cup.

"There's more." Baldric tipped his head toward the pot on the stove.

"I've had plenty, thank you. Leave your dishes in the sink, and I will do them later. I'm going to start with the upper levels."

His pale blue eyes caught mine. "Locked doors are off limits. I will not count them against you." His expression tightened. "If you attempt to bypass the locks, I will kick you out with nothing."

I smiled at him. "I understand."

But I couldn't leave part of the house grimy. Thankfully, as long as I was careful, I wouldn't need to open the doors at all.

CHAPTER 3

The upper two floors were just as neglected as the bottom two. I didn't know why Baldric hadn't made me stay in one of the cramped rooms on the fourth floor that were usually reserved for staff, but I was grateful nonetheless.

I found the cleaning supplies and started opening doors. None of them were locked, so the whole top floor needed to be cleaned. Thankfully, the manor was plumbed, so I wouldn't have to carry heavy buckets of water up three flights of steps.

I started with the ceilings and walls in each room, knocking down dust and spiderwebs from the corners and wiping down the walls. By the time I was done, the grime had settled enough in the first room to start dusting the furniture.

But first I needed to beat the dust from the mattresses.

I could haul each of them out to the tiny, frozen balcony that led to the roof, or I could... *not.*

I closed the first bedroom's door and listened to the room's song, then I pressed a hand to the mattress and coaxed the dust out into a neat pile on the floor.

By the time I had cleaned all of the mattresses, the world was a little wobbly. It had been a long time since I'd used my ability so much, and I hadn't exactly been sleeping well for the past few weeks thanks to the stress about the rent.

My energy reserves were low, but they would recover somewhat once the sun set.

I clutched the broom close as footsteps echoed up the stairwell. Had Baldric somehow sensed what I was doing? I should've waited until he was asleep.

I stumbled into the nearest bedroom and started sweeping the dust toward the door. The floor under my feet tipped and rolled, and my knuckles went white around the broom handle as I desperately tried to find my balance.

I just needed to pretend everything was fine long enough to get Baldric to leave. Then I'd sit down for a minute or two and recover.

The footsteps stopped outside the door. I moved the broom in a tiny arc and hoped I wouldn't fall on my face.

"You didn't come down for tea," Baldric said from the doorway.

I glanced up, then blinked hard when it seemed as if there were two of him standing in the hall. He was carrying a tray with a teapot and a plate filled with an assortment of tiny sandwiches.

"I didn't hear the bell," I said. "You shouldn't have troubled yourself."

He frowned at me and stepped into the room to set the tray on the narrow chest of drawers. "I promised you room and board."

"Thank you."

His sharp gaze raked over me, and his eyes narrowed. "What's wrong?"

I wiggled my fingers in a dismissive little wave without letting go of the broom. "I just overdid it a bit with all the dusting. Nothing to worry about. Thank you again for the tea."

The dismissal wasn't subtle, but Baldric ignored it. He sniffed the air and scowled. "How long has it been since you last used your magic?"

I shook my head even as the breath froze in my lungs. "Hard work isn't magic."

The icy look in his eyes pinned me in place. "How long?"

"Magic isn't real," I denied with a laugh that felt far too brittle.

He stepped closer, and I scrabbled for the knife in my apron. Unfortunately, upon releasing the broom, I lost the one thing that had been helping me balance. The floor tipped, and I tilted directly into Baldric's waiting arms.

When I struggled, he set me back on my feet but kept his hands on my shoulders. I drew the knife with shaking fingers. "Magic isn't real," I repeated. "I'm not a witch."

He let go of me with one arm and yanked up his left sleeve, sending the button flying and revealing a strong forearm. "Cut me."

"What? No!" I winced at the instinctive response and added threateningly, "I mean, I will if you don't let me go."

"If magic isn't real, then the blade will cut me. So cut me." When I continued to hesitate, he pried the knife from my hand with laughable ease. He held it up. "Watch."

He tapped the blade against his forearm and the metal rang like he'd knocked it against a stone. When he drew the edge across his skin, it didn't even leave a mark behind. He handed me the knife and I accepted it instinctively. "Try for yourself."

I tapped the back of the blade against his arm and it vibrated like he was made of armor instead of flesh. I tested the knife's edge. It was as sharp as I always kept it, but when I tried to make a tiny cut on Baldric's arm, the blade refused to bite in.

I dared to run a finger over his wrist, but his skin felt normal. He sucked in a breath, and I snatched my hand away. "What are you?" I whispered.

His eyes glinted and his expression closed. "A person with magic, just like you. When was the last time you used yours?"

To admit to having magic was to invite death, either from other creatures or from the king's knights. Baldric had shown me his secret to put us on even footing, but it was still difficult to force the words past my unwilling throat.

"Months ago," I murmured. "Longer since I've used this much. But I'll be fine. The tea and food will help."

He pressed me back toward the bed, and I sank down onto the mattress when my knees hit the edge. The world stabilized a bit. Sitting was lovely. I should've done it before he arrived. Maybe then he wouldn't have suspected anything.

A teacup appeared before my nose. "Here, drink."

The tea was overly sweet, and I grimaced before I could modulate the expression into something more polite. "The sugar will help you recover faster," Baldric said.

I drained the cup, but he just took it and refilled it with more syrupy tea. I drank another sip to appease him, then dipped my head. "I'm feeling much better, thank you. Don't let me keep you from your duties."

He took the cup and replaced it with a plate of tiny sandwiches. "Eat."

"You really don't have to—"

"*Eat.*"

I took a bite. Ham and cheese and apple were surprisingly delicious together. I stopped paying attention to Baldric entirely and focused on demolishing everything on my plate. The smoked salmon and cucumber sandwich—where had he gotten cucumbers in the middle of winter?—was even better.

By the time my plate was empty, I was feeling almost normal.

I stood, and the floor stayed where it was supposed to be... *mostly.* I drank the rest of the lukewarm tea and smiled at Baldric. "Thank you again. I'll be okay now."

"I will help you down to your room."

I shook my head. "I'm not done. I can dust and sweep and mop without magic. I only have a week, and I can't afford to waste time."

I did not mention that leaving the job half-finished would be worse than passing out from magic overuse, but if he insisted I return to my room, then I'd just sneak back up later tonight.

He sighed, then bent and picked up the broom I'd dropped. "You dust. I will sweep."

I stared at him in horror. "Absolutely not." I tried to snatch the broom away, but he refused to let go, and the attempt put me far too close to him.

One corner of his mouth tipped up, nearly a smile, and the hint of warmth was a dangerous distraction. Could I make that smile grow?

I mentally shook my head and tugged on the broom again. "I will clean. You go back to lording or smuggling or whatever it is you do all day."

He pulled the broom back. I refused to let go, so he ended up dragging me even closer. I growled at him, and the other corner of his mouth tipped up. "This is not a battle you will win," he murmured.

He had no idea. A secretive grin bloomed on my lips. "Are you sure?"

Some of the iciness in his eyes melted as his gaze dropped to my mouth. I was close enough to feel the heat from his chest. If I tipped my head up just a little more, I could brush my lips over his.

Desire curled through my belly. He sucked in a breath, and his expression sharpened into hunger. I wasn't the only one affected. I could pull him closer and leave the world behind for a little while.

But I had a house to clean, which meant I didn't have time for a dalliance, as much as we both might enjoy it.

While he was distracted—and before I joined him in that

state—I used my magic to call the broom from his hand. The effort left me dizzy again, but it was worth it if only for the split second of shocked surprise on his face.

Then a deep growl rumbled through the room, strong enough to rattle my bones. I froze in place and searched for the threat, only to discover that it was coming from Baldric.

Oh, shit.

Maybe I should've let him keep the broom and assume victory. My magic was good for cleaning, not for fighting. I might be able to coax dust to fly into his eyes, but that was the extent of my offensive abilities—which is why I had learned how to wield a sword.

A sword that was now two floors below me.

"Do *not* continue to use your magic unless you would like to spend the next week in bed," he snarled, biting off each word with furious temper. "You are dangerously exhausted."

He was angry because I'd overused my magic? It would almost be sweet if it wasn't also terrifying.

I shook my head to deny his words, and the floor tilted, proving that he was more correct than I would prefer. Still, I bluffed. "I'm fine."

He took a deep breath and the rumble returned. "I can smell it."

I sniffed myself, but I didn't smell anything out of the ordinary. "Maybe your nose is broken."

"Of all the frustrating—" He clamped his jaw shut before he finished the sentence, then pinned me in place with a deadly glare and pointed at the bed. "You will sit there and drink another cup of tea while I sweep."

"Or? Threats usually come with some sort of 'or else' clause."

His head tipped to the side. "Very well. Rest now or I will lock you in your room until you've recovered—*completely*."

"You could *try*," I agreed in my sweetest tone.

The rumble rose in volume until the teapot vibrated on the tray. Perhaps it was foolish, but I didn't feel like I was in danger. After all, he was trying to intimidate me into *resting*, which wasn't exactly villainous behavior.

"You can keep growling if you'd like," I said. "But I have chores to do."

His eyes narrowed and the growl abruptly cut off. He stared at me while he slowly unbuttoned his right cuff then started rolling up the sleeve. The fine white fabric was brilliant against the tan warmth of his skin.

"What are you doing?" I demanded, forcefully dragging my eyes from the captivating expanse of muscle and skin. "You are *not* helping. You'll ruin your clothes. Just go back downstairs and leave me to it."

"If you insist on continuing to clean, then I insist on helping. And as this is my house, I get to make the rules. If you don't like them, then you are welcome to leave." He raised a challenging eyebrow.

If I left now, the state of his house would be a constant prickle in the back of my mind, and from the look in his eye, he knew it, too.

"Fine," I agreed with a huff. "If you want to help, you can. What do I care if you ruin your fancy shirt?" I caught the grimace before it could escape. Dirty laundry *also* made my magic prickle, but I was trying my best not to make *every* mess in this house my problem.

Owner included.

I handed him a dusting cloth. "Dusting needs to happen before sweeping, so get started on the furniture. I'll do the rooms on the far side of the hall while you do this side." I smiled with my own challenge. "But if I determine you've done a poor job, I want you to promise you'll go away and leave me in peace."

"I'll do both sides while you sit and have another cup of tea. If I do a poor job, I will let you take over. But if you get up before I'm done, I'll help you clean the *entire* house. In my finest clothes."

When I gaped at him, he bowed with a smile that was more threat than amusement, then left the room.

CHAPTER 4

S itting while someone else cleaned was a torture all its own. I drank my tea and grumbled insults under my breath, but I didn't get up. I did, however, let a tiny bit of magic seep through the walls so I could keep track of his progress.

And he was doing a good job, dammit.

Once he was done, I would just have to sweep and mop and this level would be clean. I silently urged him to move faster.

He saved the room I was occupying for last. I curled my fingers into fists as he worked. He diligently wiped down all of the furniture before meeting my eyes. "Well?"

"You obviously *can* clean, so why don't you?"

He lifted one shoulder. "Once you reach a certain age, time flows differently. The dust accumulates between one blink and the next."

"Is that age thirty? Because you can't be much older than that, and I've yet to meet anyone else who fell to pieces so early."

Something dark and ancient crossed his face. "Thirty was a long time ago." He tipped his head to the side as he considered me. "Did no one teach you about the creatures inhabiting this world?"

"My mother did her best," I said stiffly. My father had left her pregnant and alone without ever once mentioning that he was one of said creatures. A baby witch was a horrible liability under the current king, but my mother had refused to give me back to the forest—a quaint euphemism for a terrible practice.

We'd moved every three months until I'd learned to control my magic, then every year just to be safe. I'd made every single thing about my mother's life harder, but she'd loved me with a fierceness that still stole my breath.

Losing her was a wound that wouldn't quite heal, even five years later.

I tucked away the pain and rose from my seat. "Thank you for dusting. I will take over from here."

For a moment, Baldric looked like he would argue, but in the end, he bowed slightly. "Dinner is in an hour. Don't be late. Unless you'd like my help tomorrow, too."

DESPITE MY BEST EFFORT, I was five minutes late to dinner. I was still wearing the gray dress I'd worn to clean, but I had taken the time to ditch the apron and magically pull the dirt and grime out of the fabric. The sun had set, and my magic was replenished enough that cleaning the dress had required barely any effort.

I could start on the third floor after dinner. Though maybe I should prioritize my bedroom or the room's discordant song would prevent me from sleeping well.

Baldric had covered his shirt with a dark jacket, and I mourned the loss of his bare forearms for a moment as I settled into the seat next to him.

"You're late," he murmured.

I sniffed. "I am perfectly on time. *You* were unfashionably early."

Rather than responding, Baldric lifted the silver dome

covering the large platter in front of us, revealing a rib roast and glazed carrots. My gaze darted to him in amazement. "You made this? And you're going to share it with me?"

Some emotion flashed across his face before he dipped his chin. "You are my guest."

I shook my head with a rueful smile. "I'm a servant, and an unwanted one at that."

"You are my guest," he repeated. He carved a thick slice of meat from the roast and gestured to my plate. "May I?"

I held my plate out and he put the meat on it, then did the same for himself. I served myself some carrots, then put some on his plate as well. It was weirdly intimate, serving each other food, even if it was practical.

If he shared my discomfort, he didn't show it. He poured me a glass of deep red wine. "Did you finish cleaning the fourth floor?"

"I did. After dinner, I'll clean the kitchen, then start on the third floor." I smiled. "I might get done early."

That did not elicit the relieved response I'd expected. Instead, Baldric frowned at me, his expression once again unreadable. "I hired you for a week of work."

"You hired me to clean your house," I disagreed. "I estimated a week, but since I no longer have to worry about you catching me using magic, I can get done sooner."

"No." His voice was flinty. "I want the week we agreed to."

"Why? You didn't even want to hire me in the first place."

"I also don't want you to work yourself to exhaustion. Is that so difficult to believe?"

"Honestly? Yes." My knife slid through the meat on my plate with an ease I wasn't used to from the cuts I usually bought. The first bite was bliss and the second was even better.

"If you insist on continuing to clean today, then I will help you."

"You could do that," I said slowly. "Or you could retire to

your study and smoke cigars or whatever it is that smugglers do in their free time and leave me to my job."

The corners of his eyes crinkled the tiniest bit. "So you've decided on smuggler then?"

"For now. Unless you'd care to enlighten me?"

He shook his head with the ghost of a smile, and we lapsed into silence as we ate. I couldn't quite figure him out. I'd thought he was icy and forbidding, and he was, certainly. But heat and humor lurked under his frozen exterior, and he was treating me better than any employer I'd had in the past.

After dinner, Baldric helped me clean the kitchen despite my protests. When everything was tidy, he tipped his head toward the door to the rest of the house. "I don't have any cigars, but I do have Knights & Bandits. Care for a match?"

The popular strategy game was one of my favorites, and I was good at it. I nodded slowly. "I'll play a game. But only if I get to start as bandits."

"You think a smuggler can't play knights?"

I grinned at him. "I guess we'll find out, won't we?"

CHAPTER 5

Baldric's study was cleaner than the rest of the house. It wasn't *clean*, but it was close enough not to needle my magic. I'd expected a dark den of wood and leather, but the walls were bright white, the desk was deep blue, and the seating was plushly upholstered.

And rocks, minerals, and crystals crowded every bookshelf. They sparked in the light, glittering just as brightly as the bits of quartz in the stones I'd given him. I swallowed my sadness and turned my attention to the game board.

The Knights & Bandits board was made from carved stone rather than the normal wood, and the playing pieces were heavy for their size. The bandits were dark gray, the knights were light gray, and all of the pieces had a unique weapon or shield that could be removed to indicate they were injured.

The goal of the game was to capture and defend the treasure in the middle of the board. Knights had stronger attack and defense, but they could only move in the four cardinal directions. Bandits could move diagonally and attack on the same turn if they slipped behind a knight.

Because the two sides required different strategies, games

were divided into two matches, and the players switched sides between them. If each player won once, then a third match was added with the sides chosen by a coin flip.

I could play either side equally well, but I was slightly better with knights. I'd started with bandits to give myself a stronger second match and a chance to see how Baldric played.

He barely studied the board before moving his pieces with an abrupt decisiveness that could easily be mistaken for carelessness. But it only took a couple of rounds for me to see his strategy forming.

I let him build his trap while I moved my bandits in seemingly nonsensical patterns. Once he was nearly ready, I purposefully sacrificed a piece to see if he would take the bait.

For the first time, he hesitated before moving.

"Having second thoughts about killing your bandit friends?" I asked.

"I'm not a smuggler," he said, still frowning at the board. After another long pause, he attacked the bandit I'd put in danger and removed the piece from the board.

I grinned, then neatly turned his trap against him. I won by eliminating all of the knights from the board, though it would've been slightly faster if I'd held the treasure instead.

We switched pieces and reset the board for the second match. "Shall we make a wager?" Baldric asked.

His voice was a little too casual for someone who'd just lost the first match. I eyed him suspiciously. "What kind of wager?"

"If you win, I will let you out of your promise to stay a week."

"I didn't promise that, but go on," I said.

His eyes glinted. "If I win, you'll stay *two* weeks. I'll pay you for the second week, of course. Twelve silver."

"That's not exactly incentive for me to win," I said. "The house will already be clean, which means I'll make an extra twelve silver for very little work. If I win, I want out of my nonexistent promise *and* the additional silver as a bonus."

"Very well," he agreed far too easily.

We began, and within three moves, I knew I was going to be in trouble. I'd been holding back during our first match, but so had he. His bandits slowly chipped away at my knights using strategies I'd never even *seen* before.

I knew the game was lost before half of my pieces had fallen, but I kept playing, watching his moves and adapting them for myself. I had to win the third match.

When my final knight fell, a tiny, victorious smile touched Baldric's mouth. "That's one match each. You may choose your side for the third."

I'd just gotten stomped as knights, but I wasn't so sure I'd do any better as bandits. "Knights," I murmured.

If he was surprised, he didn't show it. We reset the board and began. Rather than playing cautiously, which might have been what he expected, I threw myself into my most ridiculous strategies.

It worked... for a time.

But Baldric was a quick study, and it wasn't long before I was on the run again. I delayed the inevitable by taking out half of his bandits, but it wasn't enough to stop him.

I forfeited when it became clear I couldn't win. I chuckled at my poor fallen knights, then looked up at Baldric. "You play better than anyone I've met, which means you lost the first match on purpose. I've been hustled."

"Are you unhappy with the result?" Baldric asked quietly.

He might frown and grumble, but I bet if I asked, he'd let me out of the wager. Since I didn't really have a pressing need to return to my tiny cottage, I shook my head with a smile. "I get an extra week of room, board, and wages for hardly any work. Now that I think about it, maybe *you* were hustled."

"You play well. Your strategy is... *unique*."

I laughed. "You can say it's bad. You won't offend me. But I want a rematch at some point. It's been a while since I've lost so badly."

When Baldric waved at the board in invitation, I sighed, tempted. "I'd like to, but I still need to clean my room so I can sleep. Tomorrow?"

His chin dipped. "Whenever you'd like."

CHAPTER 6

Even after cleaning the fourth floor, the kitchen, and my temporary bedroom, the castle's messy state kept me from sleeping well. I'd been half tempted to get up in the middle of the night to keep working, but I wasn't the only creature who preferred the dark, and I wasn't sure I wanted to run into Baldric in a shadowy hallway.

Or maybe I wanted it *too much*.

Either way, I stayed in bed until the sun began to lighten the horizon, then got up and got ready for the day. As I performed my morning ablutions, the mirror revealed dark circles under my eyes. I could already picture Baldric's frosty disapproval.

I headed down to the kitchen to see what I could scrounge up for breakfast. I'd expected the room to be empty, so it was a surprise to find Baldric inside, wrist deep in bread dough. His sleeves were rolled up and his forearms flexed as he expertly kneaded the dough. The casual domesticity made my magic hum.

I did my very best not to stare.

I was not successful.

Baldric tipped his head toward the stove. "The kettle is hot if you'd like tea. I'll make breakfast once I'm done with this."

I forced myself to move past him. "I can cook, if you tell me what you were planning to make."

"Bacon and eggs, but I still need to let the hens out and collect the eggs." His gaze flickered down to my feet, clad in slippers meant to be worn inside or on a stone path, not in shin-deep snow. "Have a cup of tea. I'll get the eggs in a moment."

I washed my hands. "I can take over kneading for you. Are you making a loaf or rolls?" I asked as I nudged him aside— except he didn't move. Instead, we ended up pressed together, my right side against his left. The heat of his body seeped through my dress, melting and tempting in equal measure.

He turned to glower down at me, but the expression changed when he realized just how close I was. "Do you ever follow instructions?" he murmured.

"When it suits me," I told him honestly.

His head dipped toward mine, and my heart skipped a beat as anticipation tightened my belly. My eyes were just beginning to slide closed when he abruptly jerked himself back. A muscle in his jaw flexed, and his voice was a deep rasp when he said, "Make two loaves." Then he turned and fled out into the snow without even stopping to wash his hands.

Anticipation deflated into disappointment. I sighed and took my frustration out on the dough, kneading until it was smooth and taut under my palms. I shaped it into two loaves, and the familiar routine improved my mood and made my magic happy.

I set the loaves aside to rise then cleaned the kitchen. And still, Baldric didn't return. Had the chickens eaten him? I was tempted to go check, but perhaps he was avoiding me.

The thought stung, so I buried the hurt under a list of tasks I needed to accomplish today. If I could get the third floor clean, then maybe I would sleep better tonight.

I made myself a cup of tea and carried it with me up to the

third floor. Once again, none of the doors were locked. Most of the rooms were guest bedrooms, slightly inferior to those on the second floor, but there were also two sitting rooms, a study, and a small library.

I'd need to save my magic for the mattresses and the library, since I didn't relish the thought of dusting all of the books by hand, so I started with manual cleaning, working from the top down.

I was knocking down cobwebs in the fifth room when the bell rang to call me down for breakfast. I guess the chickens hadn't eaten him after all. Hunger warred with petulance.

Hunger won.

I wiped the worst of the dust from my face and washed my hands, but that was as much as I was willing to do. Baldric would just have to deal with my dusty dress and cobwebby hair.

I slipped down the back stairs and emerged into a kitchen that smelled *divine*. My stomach growled, and Baldric's eyebrows drew together slightly. He slid another egg onto the plate he was making, then nudged it toward me. "This is for you."

Apparently, we were going to pretend he hadn't nearly kissed me, then fled like I was a living plague. Fine. I could do that.

I picked up the plate with a murmured thanks. He'd given me three eggs, two thick slices of bacon, and a generous slice of toasted bread. The loaves I'd made were still rising, so this must be from yesterday's batch.

I set the plate on the table then poured myself a cup of water. After a moment's hesitation, I poured a second cup for Baldric.

He joined me at the table with a plate that was piled even higher than mine. We ate in stilted silence.

After our previous comfortable meals, this new awkwardness was *excruciating*.

I cleared my throat. "Was everything okay with the chickens?"

"Yes."

He didn't add anything else, and I wasn't brave enough to ask if he'd been hiding from me. I summoned a smile. "That's good. The eggs are delicious."

Baldric made a low sound that might have been agreement.

The conversation died.

I finished my food in silence. Manners dictated that I should wait for Baldric to finish before leaving the table, but sitting in silence without even food as a distraction was too much to ask.

I stood and bobbed a shallow curtsy. "Thank you for breakfast."

His gaze flashed up to mine before dropping back to the table. "There's more if you want it. Help yourself."

"No, thank you," I murmured, already moving toward the sink. I washed my dishes, then put them in the rack to dry. I'd deal with putting them away later—*much later*, once he was safely somewhere else.

I retreated up the stairs and ignored the pinch of disappointment that he hadn't asked how it was going. I made it all the way to the third-floor landing before I turned and marched back down to the kitchen.

"What is wrong with you?" I demanded as soon as I reentered the room.

Baldric was still at the table, and if the question surprised him, he didn't show it. "What do you mean?"

"Earlier, you fled like I was death itself, then you hid outside with your chickens until I left the kitchen. And when I tried to make conversation, you barely spoke to me. Have you changed your mind about having a witch under your roof?"

I couldn't quite keep the hurt out of my voice, and his frown deepened into a scowl. "Of course not."

"Then what's wrong?"

"You make me *want*…"

He trailed off, and it was my turn to frown. "Want what?"

His eyes flashed, and his heated gaze pinned me in place. *"Everything."*

CHAPTER 7

The word shivered down my spine and curled around my heart. Words tumbled around my head, pressing against each other in their bid to escape, but the only thing that came out was, "Okay."

Baldric's scowl deepened to truly epic proportions. "You don't even know what you're agreeing to."

"So tell me."

His jaw clenched and his hands curled into fists. "I can't."

"Sure you can. It's easy." I gave him my most innocent smile while internally cackling. "You just open your mouth and say, 'Everything includes bending you over this table and—'"

A deep growl rolled through the room, cutting off the rest of my sentence. I froze like a rabbit before a wolf and hoped I hadn't sorely misjudged his interest.

"You are in my employ," Baldric said, his voice tightly controlled.

"Of my own volition."

His gaze pinned me in place. "Because you need the money."

I winced and dipped my chin.

"You can't truly consent when I hold all the power."

"You'd be the first employer I've had who thought that way." I'd tried to keep my voice light, but some of my bitterness bled through.

Baldric was on his feet in an instant, his presence looming huge in the small kitchen. "Who?" he demanded.

I swallowed. "It doesn't matter. And it's not what you are thinking. They didn't *do* anything, not really."

"Protecting them only allows them to hurt others."

"So, what then? You're going to go threaten every petty, would-be noble in the surrounding area? That would make a whole new problem. Several, actually."

Baldric's smile was filled with teeth and venom. "They will listen to me."

The "or else" was very clearly implied. I narrowed my eyes at him. "You said you weren't a lord, which means you don't rule this county, which means you'll only get yourself in trouble."

His mouth tipped up into a confident smile, but he didn't contradict me. Instead, he settled and the looming presence vanished.

I didn't trust it for a second. "The new landlord already hates me. If you make his friends angry and they come looking for you, what do you think is going to happen when they find *me*?"

"They will not touch you."

The words sounded like a vow, but it wasn't one he'd be able to keep. "They won't need to touch me to ruin my life," I reminded him gently. "A few rumors, and the area will be swarming with knights."

"This place is not so easily found." He slanted an amused glance at me. "Current company notwithstanding."

I considered him with a frown. "But I walked straight here."

"And that's the reason I let you inside. You shouldn't have been able to find the manor, what more open the door."

"Is that why it was unlocked? Because that's really unsafe, you know."

He laughed, and the sound rang through the room and warmed my blood. "Anyone who finds my house and opens my door will get exactly what they deserve."

"Lunch?" I asked with a raised eyebrow.

His smile tipped toward dangerous. "In a manner of speaking."

AFTER EXTRACTING a promise that Baldric wouldn't run off *right now* to go threaten the local gentry, I went back to cleaning. There were fewer rooms on the third floor than the fourth, but they were bigger and had more furniture, so it actually took *longer* to clean.

Baldric brought me lunch, then tea, then came back in his dinner jacket and glared at me. I eyed him warily. I was *this close* to finishing the level, and if I could stretch his patience another ten or fifteen minutes, I'd be done.

"I'll be down in a minute," I tried. "You don't have to wait for me."

He raised an eyebrow and silently started removing his jacket.

I mopped faster and accidentally slopped water onto my slipper and the hem of my dress. With no time to fix it, I kept moving.

Once he started rolling up his shirt sleeves, I knew I'd have to take drastic measures. I set the mop aside. I'd never finish the rest of the rooms before he decided to "help."

I called the rest of the dirt into the mop bucket with magic.

I'd already magically cleaned the library and mattresses, so the additional effort left me woozy on my feet, but the floors gleamed, just as I'd promised.

Now I just had to deal with the mop and bucket of dirty water, and I'd be done. I reached for it, but the floor decided to lurch sideways under my feet, dumping me toward the wall.

Baldric cursed under his breath and clamped a careful hand around my elbow. He hauled me back upright. "It's okay to accept help, you know."

I frowned. "But it's my job."

This close, his icy blue eyes were softer, warmer. He smelled like wood smoke and spice, and I just wanted to lay my head on his chest and enjoy the peace for a moment.

So I did.

He stilled, but before I could pull away in embarrassment, he wrapped an arm around my back and tucked me closer. I leaned against him and listened as his heart beat slow and steady.

Half the house was clean, and I'd used a decent amount of magic today, so that incessant prickle at the back of my mind was muted. I was nearly… *content*.

How long had it been since I'd felt anything close to contentment?

I lingered for a bit longer, until my damp slipper reminded me that I was coated in grime and leaning against Baldric's pristine shirt. I jerked back hard enough that I would've toppled to the floor if Baldric hadn't caught me with the arm around my waist.

He frowned at me. "What's wrong?"

"I'm filthy!" When his frown melted into a wicked smile, I huffed at him. "Not like *that*. I'm going to mess up your dinner clothes."

"A little dirt isn't the end of the world."

"Says the man living in regal squalor," I grumbled. "It might not bother *you*, but it makes my magic itch."

His scowl returned. "Is that why you haven't been sleeping?" When I nodded, his jaw firmed, like he'd come to some decision, but he just asked, "Are you ready for dinner now?"

"I have to put the mop away, then I'll meet you downstairs."

When he left without an argument, I knew he was up to something.

CHAPTER 8

I slept in the next day, and it was only after I'd stumbled down to the ground floor for breakfast that I realized *why*: my magic was barely prickling because someone had cleaned the entryway and hall. The cobwebs had been knocked down, and the floors no longer sported muddy tracks.

In fact, the whole ground floor felt cleaner than it had yesterday. The house's magical chord was much closer to harmonious, and I no longer had to work so hard to block it out.

Baldric wasn't in the kitchen, but he'd left a plate of muffins on the table. I ate a quick breakfast then returned to the second floor. A few doors were locked, but surprisingly, Baldric's room wasn't one of them.

I knocked loudly, twice. When no one answered, I cracked the door open, then swung it wider when there was no objection from inside. Like his study, the room was bright and airy and warmer than the hallway.

It was also fairly clean. I called the remaining dust and grime into the hallway with a small pulse of magic, then did a final visual sweep to ensure I hadn't missed anything.

Most of the furniture was pale gray wood, with the exception of the massive bed that appeared to be carved from a solid block of gray and white stone. Almost without thought, I moved closer, drawn.

The sculptor must have been incredible. Mythical creatures were carved into the four posts, and each culminated with a dragon perched on top. The skill was such that I expected the little dragons to take flight at any moment.

I heard footsteps a moment before Baldric asked, "Do you like it?"

"It's magnificent. How did you get it up here?"

"Carefully," he said with a laugh.

I finally turned my attention away from the bed and blinked in surprise. Baldric was wearing a shirt and trousers made from rough, homespun fabric. He had cobwebs in his hair and a smudge of dirt on his cheek.

"You've been cleaning." My voice came out more accusatory than I'd intended.

"And you slept in."

I bristled. "I never agreed to get up at dawn every day—"

"That wasn't an accusation," Baldric interrupted. "I'm *happy* you slept in. It means your magic wasn't bothering you, and you needed the rest."

I blinked at him. "You cleaned so I would sleep?"

"I didn't realize it was bothering you so much or I would've done it sooner," he said stiffly.

Warmth filled my chest. "Thank you." I grinned at him. "But I'm still keeping all the money."

His amused chuckle followed me into the hall.

By THE END of the first week, the house was clean, my magic was content, and I'd lost a dozen matches of Knights & Bandits without a single win. The losses pricked my pride, but I *was*

improving, albeit slowly. Baldric's tactics were icy and efficient, much like the man himself, but they were learnable. In another week, I might actually win a match.

Especially if I went home and retrieved the one low-cut dress I owned.

Baldric had ignored all of my increasingly less subtle attempts at flirtation, much to my eternal frustration, but I could *feel* his eyes watching me when my back was turned. He wasn't as unaffected as he liked to pretend.

As much as I didn't want to trek through the snow for hours again, I *did* need to go check on my cottage, so I rose with the sun and dressed warmly. Low clouds were threatening the horizon, but if I moved fast, I could make it home and back before they arrived.

Baldric wasn't in the kitchen when I arrived, so I helped myself to a quick breakfast and a cup of hot tea. I lingered longer than I normally would've, but Baldric still didn't appear. He wasn't in his study, either.

I paused, torn. I'd like to let him know that I was leaving for the day, but waiting meant pushing my trip back, and I didn't relish the thought of trekking through the woods in the dark.

I tentatively tried one of the drawers in his desk. It slid open easily, but there wasn't any paper inside—at least, not any loose paper, and I certainly wasn't going to open one of the ledgers to look for some.

I finally found a stack of loose sheets in the third drawer. I took one out and carefully tore it in half, then wrote a quick note explaining my trip. I left the note on the kitchen table where he'd be sure to find it, then I let myself out into the cold morning air.

MY NEIGHBORS WERE happy to see me, and even happier that I'd found a job that paid well. The landlord hadn't tried to evict me while I was gone, and my cottage was just as I'd left it. I packed a few more clothes, then stealthily magicked away the dust that had accumulated over the last week.

By the time I was ready to return to Baldric's manor, the clouds were looming closer, and I eyed them warily. They were heavy and dark, promising a storm. I didn't want to get caught out in the open, but if I stayed in the village tonight, then I'd have to trek through even deeper snow tomorrow.

And my absence would likely worry Baldric.

I glanced at the clouds again. They hadn't moved. If I hurried, I should be able to make it before the storm hit, and then I'd get to curl up with a cozy fire—and, if I played my cards right, Baldric.

With the thought of warm fires and low-cut dresses in mind, I set off. The path out of the village was easy enough to follow, but soon the snow deepened. Luckily, I'd broken the trail on my way to town earlier, so I could follow my own footprints back.

I made good time, but the clouds made *better* time. I was a little more than halfway to the manor when the wind picked up. It sliced through my cloak and chilled my skin. My teeth started chattering, but I pressed onward.

Baldric would insist I drink some hot tea when I arrived, and that would warm me up. I just had to keep going.

But a few minutes later, as if mocking my desire for warmth, the sky opened up. I'd expected snow, which would've been inconvenient but manageable. Instead, I got freezing rain.

I was soaked to the bone in a matter of minutes. I pushed myself faster. This weather was a death sentence, and I refused to die after finding a tiny piece of contentment—the universe didn't get to be *that* cruel.

I squinted at the path. The wind and rain were making it harder to follow the trail I'd left earlier, and while sunset was still hours away, the storm had brought a false dusk that made it difficult to see.

The manor was closer than the village. I stumbled onward, determined to find it.

But despite my determination, the icy rain sapped my strength and numbed my limbs. The fifth time I fell, I could barely force myself to stand. I laughed with bitter resignation. It seemed the universe *would* get to be that cruel after all.

When a hazy, cloaked figure emerged from the gloom, I squinted. Who would possibly be out in this weather? The icy rain beaded off the figure's expensive oilskin cloak, and resentful enviousness nipped at me. I would've made it if my cloak had stopped the rain.

I rested a hand on my rapier's pommel, only to frown when I realized I couldn't really feel it. My fingers were numb, and if this turned out to be a bandit, I'd have precious little defense.

Of course, what kind of bandit decided to rob people in the middle of a freezing rain storm?

That puzzle distracted me long enough for the figure to close the distance between us. I shouldn't have let them get so close, but my thoughts were slow and thick and scattered.

The cloak's hood tipped back and Baldric's scowl arrowed into me, angrier than I'd ever seen it. Why was he out in this storm?

"Am I close to the manor?" I asked.

"Not close enough." He shrugged off his cloak and flinched as the icy rain drenched him.

The action was strange enough to shock me out of the hazy half consciousness I'd been slipping into. "Don't you have any sense?" I demanded, reaching for the oilskin. "You'll die like that!" I smacked his hands away, then draped the thick cloth over his head and shoulders.

I pulled him closer, trying to clasp the cloak closed before he got any wetter, but my mitten-covered fingers were too stiff to work the toggles.

Baldric stared at me, his pale blue eyes as icy as the weather around us. "I was going to give it to you."

"I appreciate the thought, but it wouldn't help if we're not close to the manor. I'm already drenched." I looked over his shoulder. "Where's your horse?"

"Horses don't like me."

I blinked, thrown. "Then how'd you get out here? Surely you didn't walk out in the middle of a storm."

He shook his head. "I flew."

That didn't make any sense. I poked him, and he felt real enough, but I wasn't exactly in the best state to judge.

His eyebrows drew together. "What are you doing?"

"I'm trying to decide if you're real," I told him. "But I suppose it doesn't matter. If you flew here, then fly on home before you catch your death."

"Can you ride?"

I stared up at him and blinked the rain from my eyes. "I thought horses didn't like you."

"I suppose not," he murmured. He sighed, then spun the oilskin off his shoulders again and wrapped it around me before I could protest. "Don't move."

"You sure are bossy," I grumbled. "I should've imagined someone nicer."

He didn't bother with a response. He stepped back and bright light flickered through the gloom. When I could see again, a huge, pale blue dragon was crouched where Baldric had been.

Huh.

Now we were getting somewhere. I probably should've been worried that my brain was far enough gone that it had started imagining mythical creatures, but I couldn't be bothered. An interesting death was better than a lonely one.

I stepped forward and the dragon rumbled at me. "Shush. I've never petted a dragon, even an imaginary one, so I'm going to do that before I die." Belatedly, I tacked on, "If you don't mind."

The rumbling ceased, so I took that as permission and pressed a hand against the dragon's scaly blue side. After a moment, warmth bled through my soaked mittens. The scales were warm, even in the icy rain, and denser than stone. I leaned against them and willed the warmth to transfer faster. I'd read somewhere that people freezing to death often felt warm right at the end, so I guess my time was about up.

What a whimsical way to go.

Then the dragon moved and the cold rushed back in. I grumbled in annoyance, but the grumble turned into an alarmed shout when one clawed foot wrapped tight around my body. Being eaten alive was definitely less pleasant that freezing to death.

I struggled, but I couldn't escape its clutch, and the effort cost most of my remaining energy. Adrenaline could only do so much, and the cold was winning.

The claws flexed around me, as if ensuring I was truly caught. They weren't crushing, but they weren't exactly comfortable, either. Before I could figure out how to break free, the dragon launched itself into the air, and my stomach dropped to the rapidly disappearing ground.

CHAPTER 9

I lay stiff and still in the dragon's claws, trying not to do anything that would cause it to drop me. Though, perhaps falling to my death would be better than being eaten.

Fortunately or otherwise, I was likely going to freeze to death before either option became a real concern. The dragon had tucked me close, shielding me from the worst of the rain, but I couldn't feel most of my body, and thoughts flitted through my head without ever sticking. I should've been terrified, but even that emotion felt too far away, ephemeral and fleeting.

I don't know how long we traveled before I was set on the hard, snowy ground with more care than I expected. I was still trying to pry my eyes open when someone with strong arms—strong *human* arms—scooped me up.

The light behind my eyelids brightened, and the air no longer stung my lungs. We were inside. I cracked my eyes open, but all I could see was the wet, dark tunic of whoever was carrying me.

"Don't let the dragon eat me," I whispered.

A brief grunt vibrated against my cheek, and a deep voice murmured, "You would hardly be a satisfying meal."

I snorted softly. At least I had that going for me.

I finally roused myself enough to protest when I was laid on a soft mattress. "My clothes are wet."

"I'll dry them in a second."

The familiarity of the voice was enough to get me to crack my eyes open again. Baldric was leaning over me, a frown on his face. I reached for him, but my arm wasn't entirely under my control and it fell back before I made contact.

"Are you a dragon?" I whispered.

He met my eyes. "Yes."

That was not the answer I'd expected. "Promise you won't eat me."

"People are not as delicious as you seem to think you are." When I just stared at him, he sighed. "I promise I won't eat you."

"Thanks," I breathed, letting my eyes slide closed. Then I roused myself again and added, "Even after I'm dead."

"You're not going to die." As if to prove his point, warmth flooded through me, chasing away the chill.

"How are you doing that?"

"Magic."

"Magic isn't real," I mumbled reflexively.

The corner of his mouth curled. "Neither are dragons. Or witches."

"That's true." My eyes slid closed as the warmth spread. "Is that why you weren't worried about me cutting you?"

"Yes."

There was something off about his tone. "Are you mad at me?"

"Furious," he agreed, his voice a low rumble.

I pried my eyes open long enough to scowl at him. "I was trying to get back to you so we could sit in front of the fire, and I could distract you with my new dress."

"If I hadn't found you, you would've *died.*" Now that I was listening for it, I could hear the quiet fury laced through the words.

"But you *did* find me."

"I was nearly too late. What were you thinking?"

I hissed as his magic washed away the numbness in my fingers. The pain was sharp but thankfully brief as he continued to heal me.

"I was thinking that if I didn't return, you'd worry and do something dangerous like going out in a storm. And I was *right*."

"You will not risk yourself for me again," he demanded.

"Bossy," I grumbled around a yawn. The last of the cold was fading and weariness was creeping in.

"If that's what it takes to keep you safe, then yes."

"That's okay," I murmured as sleep pulled me under, "I like you even when you're bossy."

He tucked the blankets around my now warm and dry form, then whispered softly, "I like you, too. Far too much."

He stood to leave and as much as I wanted to chase him down and demand answers, my body had other ideas.

I was asleep before his footsteps faded.

I AWOKE to a roaring fire and an empty room. My clothes were stiff, and I still had my boots on—*in bed!!*—but otherwise, I felt fine. I got up carefully so the rapier strapped to my waist wouldn't poke me *or* the mattress.

Baldric had left his nice oilskin cloak, probably because it'd been wrapped around me. I magically pulled the dirt and grime from it and set it aside to return. The effort left me woozier than I would've preferred, so I decided on a warm bath for myself. I'd deal with my clothes later.

After I was clean and dressed, I went to find Baldric—and breakfast. My first stop was the kitchen. Baldric was slicing onions into a heavy pot, and based on the stinging in my eyes, he'd been doing it for a while.

He tipped his head toward the table without pausing. "There's a plate for you."

His tone was hard to read, and his expression gave nothing away. I narrowed my eyes at him. "Did I imagine that you were a dragon?"

The knife stilled for a fraction of a second before resuming. "You did not imagine it."

I wiggled my fingers, all perfectly healthy and still attached to my hands. "And you healed me."

"I did."

"Thank you." I considered the tense set of his shoulders and the furrow between his eyebrows. "Are you still mad at me?"

His glittering gaze pinned me in place. "I'm still furious that you nearly died, yes."

"You should come with me next time. You know, to keep me out of trouble. And then I won't worry you if I have to stay overnight."

The knife slammed into the cutting board with rattling force. "You would invite *a dragon* home with you?"

"I would invite *you* home with me. Is that a problem?"

His glare was hot enough to burn. "I'm dangerous. And your employer."

I could fix one of those easily enough. "Fine, I quit." I held up a hand to ward off the argument I could see brewing in his expression. "I promised to *stay* for two weeks, I didn't promise to clean for those two weeks. So unless you object, I'll spend the next week as your guest, not your employee."

The manor was already clean. It would take the barest hint of magic to keep it that way, and what Baldric didn't know wouldn't hurt him.

He stared at me for a long moment. I held my breath. It was possible I was reading the whole situation wrong, and he'd refuse to let me stay as a guest. Finally, he set the knife aside. "I will get the wages you are owed. Now eat."

I barely contained the sigh of relief. "I will, thank you."

The covered plate held an assortment of delicate pastries that would've taken him all night to make. Had he stayed up, or had he somehow gotten to the village and back this morning?

Sweet, flaky dough surrounded a dark jam filling. The first bite revealed the jam was blackberry, and it was just tart enough to balance the dough's sweetness. If he'd made these, then he could make a fortune by opening a bakery.

I was working my way through my second pastry when Baldric returned. He set twenty-four silver on the table. "Your wages." Then he placed a gold crest next to the silver. "And a bonus for a job well done. Your employment is now finished. You may stay as my guest, if you would like, or you may return to the village. If you wish to return, I will take you to the edge of town."

He'd paid me for both weeks. I *should* give him the extra dozen silver back, but I needed it more than he did. I swiped the silver into my hand, then pushed the gold crest back toward him. "I would like to buy back my rocks."

Something ancient and feral flashed across his face before he shook his head. "That's impossible."

Unexpected pain lanced through my chest. "Why? Did you already get rid of them? Were they not good enough for your collection?"

"They already *are* part of my collection," Baldric said. "That's the problem. It would be very difficult for me to give them to you, but I can *loan* them to you."

"Then I will loan you this gold crest as collateral."

Baldric shook his head. "It wouldn't be even. If part of my collection is ever taken out of the manor, I could find it anywhere in the world, but if you give me this gold, you wouldn't be able to find it again if I hid it. Keep it. It's yours."

"You can find the rocks anywhere? Even if I travelled across the continent?" When he nodded, I asked, "How?"

"Magic."

"So you'll always be able to find me?"

His expression was unreadable. "As long as you remain with part of my collection, yes. Does that bother you?"

I smiled softly. "No, it doesn't bother me at all."

CHAPTER 10

After breakfast, Baldric retrieved my collection, and I spent some time arranging the various pieces on the vanity in my room. The purple geode was my best piece, and it sparkled in the light from the window. Baldric had kept every single stone, even the ones that were merely sentimental to me, and my heart brimmed with warmth.

I wandered through the house, subtly pulling residual dust from the rooms. I'd quit, and I'd meant it, but a guest doing a little tidying wasn't strange, right? Especially when it made the house's song ring clear and cheerful.

I stepped out of the third-floor library and nearly ran into Baldric. I jerked to a stop and swayed backward. He caught my shoulder to prevent me from stumbling.

"Oh, sorry," I said, "I didn't see you there."

"What are you doing?"

His glare was back, so I lifted my chin. "Nothing that concerns you."

"You are a guest, and guests don't clean."

"I'm a guest, so I can do what I want," I countered.

A low rumble rose in his chest, and I reached for him before I thought better of it. The sound vibrating against my palms was like a purring cat, only on a much larger scale. I peeked up at him, but he didn't seem upset, so I tried pushing my luck just a little further.

"Will you show me your dragon form again?"

"Most people run away screaming when they encounter a dragon." He dropped a pointed glance to my hands, but covered them with his own when I would've snatched them away. "You tried to pet me. Why is that?"

I winced. "Sorry about that. I was half convinced I was imagining you so I wouldn't die alone." When his glare deepened into dangerous territory, I rushed to add, "You've been nothing but kind to me. Why would I fear you?"

One eyebrow winged up. "Because I'm a dragon?"

"I did *briefly* wonder if you were going to eat me, but since I remain uneaten, I'm not too worried about it."

The rumble in his chest dipped into a lower octave as his eyes narrowed. The sound drew me like a moth to flame. I wanted to press my entire body against his to feel the vibration. I settled for glancing up at him, then letting my gaze drift to his mouth with pointed interest.

His hands tightened over mine, but he didn't move.

His expression, however, blazed with heat.

"You're no longer my employer. I'm a guest, here of my own free will. If I kiss you, are you going to eat me after all?"

One side of his mouth tipped up into a wicked smile. "You might enjoy it."

My smile matched his. "Why don't we find out?"

His head dipped, then his lips were on my mine, firm yet gentle, and my world narrowed until it only held the two of us and the places where we touched. Our breath mingled and sparks shivered down my spine. His heart beat steady and strong under my palms, and the rumble in his chest deepened until I could feel it in my bones.

I pressed closer, fitting my mouth to his, and he groaned low in his chest before carefully drawing away, his breathing harsh. He stared at me, a furrow on his forehead. "Have I enchanted you? I thought you were safe because you have magic of your own, but perhaps I was wrong."

I was more concerned with the shape—and feel—of his lips than what he was saying, so it took a moment for the words to sink through the hazy cloud of pleasure. "What do you mean?"

His hands fell away from me, breaking our remaining connection, and I nearly reached for him before remembering that he was putting distance between us on purpose.

"Dragons can *lure* humans, for the lack of a better word. Sometimes intentionally, but often *accidentally*. It's a survival mechanism. You might only want me because my magic is enchanting you."

I laughed, then laughed harder when he scowled in offense. "I'm sorry," I gasped with a placating wave. "I'm not laughing *at* you. I'm laughing because you think I kissed you due to some sort of dragon magic. I can't be enchanted. You're welcome to try if you don't believe me, but I'll warn you, the last creature who tried was *very* upset when it didn't work."

That wiped all expression from Baldric's face and a dangerous intensity took its place. "*Who* tried *what?*" he demanded softly.

"I found a woman in a pond. Except it wasn't a woman at all, and when she tried to lure me into the water, I refused. I could feel her magic, but it slid over me without sticking. She was furious. I guess I was supposed to be her next meal. I offered to get her food from the village, but she just cursed at me until I was forced to leave. When I went back, she was gone."

"You *went back* to a water nymph's pond?" Baldric snarled in disbelief.

I shrugged. "She seemed hungry. And I know what it's like to be alone and hungry."

He pressed one hand to his eyes while the other clenched in a fist. "I'm not going to be able to let you out of my sight, am I?" he murmured, almost to himself.

"It's not that bad. Everything worked out." I paused, then stared at his chest and murmured, "But I wouldn't mind having you around." I peeked up at him. "You know, just in case."

His gaze bored into mine. "You can't be enchanted?"

"Nope."

"So you kissed me…" he trailed off.

"Because I wanted to."

He stared at me for a moment longer, judging my sincerity, then his control snapped. His arms banded around my back as he hauled me closer, then his mouth was on mine, fierce and demanding, and oh so delicious.

I moaned and sucked his bottom lip between mine before gently raking my teeth over it. His palm cupped my jaw, tipping my head to the side so he could return the favor. I clung to his shoulders, his neck, and time lost all meaning.

I was unprepared when he jerked back with a deep inhale and a muttered curse. I blinked at him. "What's wrong?"

"Dinner is burning."

"You can tell that from here?"

"Yes. Being able to smell smoke from great distances is helpful when your enemies can breathe fire."

"Can *you* breathe fire?"

His head cocked to the side. "Of course."

I huffed out a breath. "So dragons can breathe fire, but all my magic does is pester me when a house is untidy? Seems unfair."

Baldric smiled. "Hearth magic is more powerful than you might think. You can turn a house into a happy home—or a terrifying nightmare."

"Terrifying enough to get a landlord to stop being horrible to his tenants?"

Baldric's eyes narrowed. "That's a very specific example."

I shrugged noncommittally and turned to go rescue our dinner, but Baldric caught my hand. "Tell me."

I tugged him into motion, unwilling to let the landlord steal our dinner in addition to everything else. By the time we'd made it to the kitchen, I'd given him a brief overview of the situation, and Baldric's growl was back—and scary. Gone was the enticing rumble, and in its place was a sound that raised the hair on my arms.

I could finally smell the burning scent in the air. Baldric arrowed straight for the oven and pulled out two deeply browned loaves of bread. The top edges of the ears were blackened, and the smell of burning bread grew stronger. The loaves were fine, but another few minutes would've meant no bread for dinner.

"How did you smell that from upstairs?"

Baldric shrugged as he transferred the loaves to a rack to cool. "Magic."

It still stunned me how easily he spoke about magic. But I suppose if I could turn into a giant, fire-breathing dragon, I wouldn't be too worried, either.

Once the bread was safe, Baldric turned back to me and our previous conversation. "Your magic likely *could* terrify your landlord into better behavior, but it would take time, and you'd need to stay close to do it. It would be much faster for a dragon to land on his roof and threaten to burn his house to the ground if he didn't reconsider."

"Wouldn't that bring the king's knights down on you?"

A lethal smile touched Baldric's mouth. "Only if he is unwise."

I snorted. "He is."

"Then he will learn why dragons are not to be trifled with."

Worry pinched my belly. Baldric was undoubtedly powerful, but the king had a legion of knights. And once they came seeking the dragon, they'd overrun the village. If any of the other villagers were hiding magic—as I suspected more than a few *were* —then they'd be in danger, too. I shook my head. I couldn't risk it.

Baldric closed the distance between us. "What are you thinking?"

"Knights in the village would be a disaster. We need to drive off the landlord—or change his mind—without revealing our magic."

"Or I could kill him." At my shocked expression, Baldric's growl returned. "He planned to evict you in the middle of winter. My sympathy for him is nonexistent."

"True enough," I admitted. "But maybe we try something less permanent first. If that doesn't work, you can eat him."

CHAPTER 11

The freezing rain had stopped and the skies were clear and blue, but I still didn't relish yet another hike through knee-deep snow—even if Baldric had given me a fur-lined oilskin that kept the wind from reaching my skin.

At least I'd have company for this trip.

Baldric slanted a glance at me as we stepped out into the bitter air. "Were you telling the truth about wanting to see my dragon form again?"

I beamed and clasped my hands together to keep from reaching for him. "I was. Are you going to show me?"

"It'll be faster if I fly us to the village."

My nose wrinkled. "How much faster? Because your claws weren't exactly comfortable."

"Since you're not freezing to death this time, you can ride."

My smile tipped into perfect innocence. "Are you inviting me to ride you, my lord dragon?"

Baldric's face darkened with hunger, and his fists clenched. "Let me kill the landlord and be done with it, then you can ride me as often as you'd like," he growled.

It was certainly tempting with Baldric's body taut with longing, but I sighed in resignation. "We should at least *try* not to murder him. Talking to his secretary is a good place to start."

Baldric grumbled something under his breath, then pinned me in place with a glare. "In that case, *behave*, my lady witch."

I grinned at him. "I don't think I will."

"Witch," Baldric growled, and it sounded like an endearment, prayer, and admonishment all wrapped into one. "Once I transform, I won't be able to speak, but I'll still understand you, so if you get frightened, let me know."

"I won't be."

Baldric didn't look convinced, but he didn't argue. "You will be able to sit just in front of my wings. I won't let you fall. But if you're not comfortable, I can carry you in my claws."

"I'll make it work," I promised. "I don't need to be carted around like a tasty sheep."

"So you *don't* want to be eaten?" Baldric asked with such a straight face that it took me a solid second to believe my ears.

Desire flushed up my body, and I shivered. "*Now* who needs to behave?"

"You're a bad influence."

"True enough, but you're stalling. Change, dragon. I promise I won't run away screaming."

"That's because you have no self-preservation instinct at all," Baldric grumbled. But he backed away, putting space between us. After another long look at me, his magic flashed and I blinked. When my eyes opened, a pale blue dragon crouched where Baldric had been standing before.

Even crouching on his four solid legs, he was as tall as the manor's first story, and the wings tucked against his back looked like they could blot out the sky. Two sharp horns swept back from his long, pointed head, and despite the cold, his breath didn't fog the air.

In fact, he blended into the wintry landscape far better than something his size should've.

"Can you really breathe fire?" I dared to ask.

That rumbling growl he sometimes made was deeper in this form. He turned his head carefully away from me and flame sprouted from his mouth, melting the snow in a wide path before him.

"Well that's a delight," I murmured in quiet awe. "No more shoveling snow for me."

Baldric snorted, then tipped his head toward his back. He crouched deeper so his left foreleg could be used as a stepladder.

I clambered up his side, then paused to lean against the firm warmth of his scales. "How are you so warm?" He made a sound that was impossible to interpret, so I guessed, "Magic?"

He nodded.

I climbed the rest of the way up and swung my leg over his shoulder, sitting where his long neck met his body. Sharp, armored spikes ran down the back of his neck, but they flattened into warm, slightly rough scales just ahead of where I was seated, so I was surprisingly comfortable.

I gripped him with my knees, and his wings were tucked just behind my calves. As long as he didn't do anything *too* extreme, I could likely keep my seat.

When he rumbled a question, I sucked in a surprised breath as the vibration buzzed straight between my legs.

I'd certainly felt *that*.

Then he took a few tentative steps and his scales shifted as his muscles bunched and moved. The slight ridges rubbed against me with tiny flashes of pleasure.

Oh no. I didn't realize I'd whimpered the words until Baldric froze. His head swiveled back toward me, and he chuffed out another wordless question that stoked the fire higher.

Then he took a deep breath and went rigidly still before a deep growl vibrated through his body—and mine.

"If you don't stop that," I gasped out, "then we're not going to make it to the village."

The growl deepened, and I squirmed, trying to escape and get closer at the same time. Magic flared and I had a single moment of weightlessness before Baldric caught me in his arms—his *human* arms.

I blinked at him, disoriented. "What—"

His lips covered mine in a kiss that was as hot as it was tender. When he finally pulled back, we were both breathing hard. "The village can wait," he half demanded, half pleaded.

When I nodded in wordless agreement, he shouldered us back into the manor and climbed the stairs to his room.

We didn't leave again until well past dinner.

THE NEXT DAY, when we finally managed to behave long enough to get into the air, I marveled at the strong beat of Baldric's wings and the rapidly disappearing ground. Rather than wading through deep snow for hours, the trip took mere minutes, and I was kept warm by Baldric's body and my new oilskin.

"I could get used to traveling like this," I told him as soon as we'd landed.

His eyes glinted with wicked delight. "You can rid—"

I pressed my gloved fingers to his lips. "Behave, dragon."

"Never, witch," he murmured, nipping at my mittens.

I grabbed his hand and pulled him into motion before we could get distracted—*again*. We'd landed at the edge of town, hidden by Baldric's magic, so it was a short walk to the landlord's secretary's office.

When I carefully hinted at what we were doing, the secretary let us look at the landlord's books and correspondence without even needing a bribe.

I gave him one anyway.

The solicitor a few doors down was a little more reticent, but a gold crest changed her mind. Apparently Lord Saario had neglected to pay her salary since the estate had transferred into his name, so she wasn't *technically* in his employ.

Since Baldric and I now *were* her employers—kind of—she let us use her meeting room. We settled down with the books and papers, and there, laid out in black and white, was the reason Lord Saario was so desperate to pull in more rent. Evidently the young lord enjoyed gambling and had accumulated quite the debt before serendipitously inheriting.

But the previous landlord had been very fair to his tenants, and most of the estate's value was in the land and the relation-ships, not in the bank.

The creditors who'd been promised payment in full as soon as the estate settled weren't interested in tenant relationships or unsalable land. Lord Saario was out of time. In fact, even if Baldric and I did nothing at all, I would still likely have a new landlord in the spring.

But the villagers would suffer this winter as they tried to make untenable rents.

I froze as I reread the letter in my hand. Perhaps the old landowner's passing hadn't been quite so much *serendipitous* as *schemed.* I passed the letter to Baldric. "Lord Saario killed the old landowner. Or had him killed. It's unclear."

Baldric frowned as he read. "This was with the papers the solicitor gave you?"

"Yes. And I'm going to be really upset if she knew about it and did nothing."

"Let's go ask her."

I nodded, and together we returned to the solicitor's office. Her lips pressed into a thin line when we entered. "I've helped as much as I can," she said before I could speak.

"Did you know about this?"

I handed her the letter. She glanced at it, then her eyes widened, and she read it more slowly. "Where did you get this?"

"From the papers you gave us. It was with the estate transfer stuff."

Her gaze snapped up to me. "I've never seen this before. But the paperwork was scattered over Lord Saario's desk, and he was in a hurry for me to leave because he had another appointment. When he gathered the papers, he must've included this by mistake."

"That's a pretty damning mistake," Baldric said.

The solicitor nodded. "It makes me wonder what else he's hiding." Her fingers tightened around the paper, and she leveled a surprisingly fierce glare at me. "It would be disastrous for knights to start poking around in the village. I'm sure I don't need to explain why to *you*."

The emphasis was subtle but unmistakable. When my eyes widened in understanding, she nodded very slightly. Her gaze flickered over my shoulder and a furrow appeared between her brows. I felt the tiniest shift in the air, like the heavy potential before a thunderstorm, and Baldric grunted. "I wouldn't," he advised, his voice mild.

She tipped her head to the side, and the feeling disappeared. "So you both understand why a slew of curious knights would be unfortunate."

"Does the estate *have* to pass to a family member?" I asked.

"Yes, but it doesn't have to be the next closest relation. The previous Lord Saario planned to give the estate to the current lord's younger sister, but he never got around to updating his will —despite my many attempts."

"So we just need the current lord to sign over the estate to his sister."

The solicitor snorted. "Good luck. Even if he can't sell it, it's still valuable."

"More valuable than his life?" I asked.

She chuckled bitterly. "Based on everything I've seen and heard? Yes."

CHAPTER 12

The solicitor wasn't wrong. The deeper we dug into Lord Saario's life, the more we found to dislike. But for all that he was terrible, he was also *stubborn*.

Baldric taught me how to use my magic to affect a house's song in such a way that the people inside felt entirely unwelcome in their own home. Then, every night for two weeks, I snuck into Lord Saario's house with a grumbling dragon on my heels and applied what I'd learned.

On the fifteenth day, Lord Saario broke and called for his solicitor.

The sulky young lord didn't even question why the solicitor already had ownership transfer papers drawn up—or why Baldric and I were also present—he just signed everything set in front of him with barely a glance.

When he ran out of paper, Lord Saario perked up. "That's it?" he asked. "It's my sister's problem now?"

I didn't think I could like the young man less, and yet. From Baldric's quiet, rumbling growl, he didn't care much for Lord Saario, either.

"Your sister is now the official landowner," the solicitor confirmed.

Baldric's magic rose, and the young lord abruptly dropped into unconsciousness. The solicitor didn't even blink.

She calmly handed me one of the pages from the stack. "Here's his confession. I'll ensure Lady Saario is notified of the change and of her brother's crimes. The knights might do a cursory investigation, depending on how loudly Lord Saario complains, so I've warned the relevant parties to be aware."

I did not miss her pointed look. "We'll be careful."

Baldric stood and picked up Lord Saario like a sack of grain. The young man's skin was pale and waxy, and he had dark circles under his eyes, but I couldn't dredge up even a drop of sympathy.

We left the solicitor's office with the help of Baldric's magic. As we headed for the trees, he asked, "Do you want to come to the capital with me?"

My nose wrinkled. I loved flying, but the trip would take several hours, and it was *cold*. Plus, I didn't want to be anywhere near the king or his knights. "You're sure you'll be okay on your own?" I asked instead of answering.

"I'll be okay, but I'll be *better* if I know you're waiting for me, warm and safe."

I nodded and handed him the confession. "Then I'll stay and start on dinner while you deal with Saario." I pointed a stern finger at him. "Do *not* antagonize any knights while you're away."

His teeth gleamed with his smile. "But what if I need a little snack?"

EVERY FLIGHT MADE me just love the air more, and when Baldric landed in front of the manor's heavy front door, I was tempted to tell him that I'd changed my mind about the trip.

Between the oilskin and his body heat, the cold barely bothered me.

But I had other plans, so I slid from my seat and pressed a kiss against one of the scales on his neck. "Be careful."

He rumbled an affirmative at me, then waited for me to step back before picking up Saario in one massive claw. With a sweep of wings and magic, Baldric launched himself into the air.

I watched until he was out of sight.

The temperature was a lot less pleasant without a dragon to keep me warm, so I hurried inside, and my magic hummed happily as I crossed the manor's threshold. I was getting stronger now that I was using my magic more often, and I could keep the entire house clean without having to visit the individual floors or rooms.

I tidied up and worked on dinner, then I went to change into the dress I'd retrieved from my cottage but hadn't yet had an opportunity to wear.

Tonight, I was going to win, one way or another.

I'D BRUSHED my hair until it shone, and now I was in Baldric's study attempting to read, but mostly I was listening for the front door. The moment it swung open, I tugged my dress lower, smoothed down my hair, and returned my attention to the book in my hand.

Baldric approached the study with unerring accuracy, but he paused at the door. A low rumble rolled through the room. "Zenira?"

I blinked and looked up in faux surprise, as if I hadn't been aware of him since he'd arrived. "Yes?"

"What are you wearing?"

A smile curled over my lips despite my attempt to contain it. "Oh, this?" I shifted, and my cleavage threatened to escape its confines. *Perfect.* "This is the dress I went to retrieve the day I got caught out in the rain."

I gestured to the Knights & Bandits board I'd set up. "Care for a game before dinner?"

When I peeked at him, Baldric's gaze was heroically on my face, but it kept slipping lower. "Whatever you'd like," he agreed.

I pressed my lips together to hold in a laugh when he nearly tripped on an end table while crossing the room. I'd set up the board so I would be playing bandits first—and so Baldric would have an excellent view of my chest.

I leaned forward to adjust the pieces as he settled into his chair, and he groaned low in his throat. I smiled serenely. "How about a little wager?"

His gaze sharpened. "What did you have in mind?"

"If I win, I get to move in and stay as long as I want."

He swallowed, and his voice was rough when he asked, "And if I win?"

"What do you want?"

"You."

"Okay."

The arms of his chair creaked as his hands tightened around them. "You don't know what you're agreeing to."

"I trust you."

His eyes flashed and magic curled around me like a cozy blanket. "Careful, witch."

"Do we have a deal, dragon?"

He nodded, and we began playing. After a few moves, I fanned my face, and asked, "Is it warm in here?"

Before he could answer, I popped the first button on my straining bodice. He moved his piece without looking at the board.

I was winning tidily when Baldric decided to employ my own tactics against me. He stood and removed his jacket, leaving him clad in a thin linen shirt. During my next move, he slowly rolled up his sleeves, revealing his forearms.

I swallowed and barely avoided moving directly into the trap he'd laid. Then I retaliated by tracing a finger along the edge of my bodice while he considered the board—or tried to.

I narrowly won the first game, and we traded pieces.

As I was getting ready to move, Baldric removed his shirt. After I finished gaping at him, I tipped my chin up and raised my eyebrows. "So that's how it's going to be?"

His smile was deliciously wicked. "What? It's hot in here. You said so yourself."

My smile matched his. "So I did." I already knew where I was moving, so I spent a few moments ogling Baldric's chest while biting my lip. When his hands clenched, I set my piece in place. "Your move."

"Witch."

I grinned. "Dragon."

When the tide of the game started turning against me, I waited until it was Baldric's turn, then stood. "It *is* hot in here," I murmured. I'd found that my magic could affect clothing if I concentrated hard enough. With a spike of power, my dress slithered to the floor, leaving me clad in a nearly sheer chemise and half corset.

Baldric's growl shook the pieces on the board. One of his bandits shifted far enough to count as a move. "I see you've played, so it's my turn."

He didn't even glance at the board.

I leaned over and considered my options. The arm of his chair snapped under his hands with a sharp, shrill note. I magically fixed it and smoothed the room's melody back into harmony.

"You're getting stronger."

"I am," I agreed. I made my move, then met his eyes with a

coy look. "I can remove my chemise without removing the corset first. Want to see?"

"Yes." The word sounded like it was ripped from somewhere deep in his chest.

"Okay." I returned my attention to the game.

"Zenira," he growled.

I studied the board. Even with all of my distractions, I was still going to lose. But it was going to be close.

My chemise joined my dress on the floor. The half corset wasn't as comfortable without the extra layer of fabric, but the minor discomfort was worth it for the fiery heat burning in Baldric's eyes.

I smiled saucily at him. "Make your move, dragon."

He stood so quickly he bumped the table, toppling the pieces. "I forfeit. You win." He rounded the table and scooped me up, and I laughed in delight even as I snuggled against the warmth of his bare chest.

I cupped his cheek and turned his face down to mine. "Since I won, does that mean I get to move in and stay as long as I want?" He'd agreed to the wager, but I wanted to ensure he'd *meant* it.

His expression softened, and his arms tightened. "Yes. I'll help you move in whenever you're ready. And then I'm going to do everything in my power to ensure you want to stay forever. You're mine, witch."

I smiled at him and pressed my promise against his lips. "And you're mine, dragon."

EPILOGUE

The day after Baldric moved all of my furniture into his
—now *our*—room, he unlocked one of the doors that
had remained closed all through my visit and threw it
open like a magician performing a trick. A look inside revealed…
rocks.

So. Many. Rocks.

Shelves and shelves filled with stones and minerals and
gemstones of all shapes, sizes, and kinds. Few of them appeared
to be inherently valuable, just like my collection. A smile broke
across my face. "You really *do* collect rocks."

"Yes." He paused. "Are you disappointed?"

I laughed. "No. I'm *delighted*. I *love* rocks. I was heartbroken
when I had to sell mine." I took a step through the door, then
stopped and glanced at him. "Is it okay if I look around?"

"Of course."

Baldric knew the story of every item in his collection, from
the tiniest pebble to the giant piece of rose quartz in the center
of the room which he'd *liberated* from the king's own castle.

Most of them he'd found himself, but a few—like my collection—he'd bought from someone desperate to sell. My dragon

might appear icy on the outside, but he was delightfully soft at heart.

"It must've taken a lifetime to collect all of this," I murmured idly.

"More than one. Dragons live a long time."

My attention snapped to him, and anxiety twisted in my chest. Would I grow old and gray while he remained the same? "What about witches?"

"It depends."

That was not reassuring. I hadn't *exactly* discussed it with him yet, but deep in my heart, I'd already decided that he was it for me. I wanted to spend my life with him, but how would that work if I aged and died while he continued on? That would be heartbreaking for us both.

He drew me close and smoothed his thumb over my cheek. "What are you thinking?"

"I was planning to keep you as long as you'd let me, but what if I don't age like a dragon?"

He smiled softly. "You can keep me as long as you'd like. You're my mate, the other half of my soul. And I can tie your life to mine, if you're willing."

"Will that make your life shorter?" I asked with a frown. I didn't want to extend my life at the expense of his.

"No, but the mating is *permanent*. Your life will literally be tied to mine."

"So if you die, I'll die too?" When he nodded warily, I sighed in relief. "Good. I wouldn't want to live forever without you anyway."

"You have to be sure, Zenira. And we don't need to decide today."

"You were mine the moment you tried to intimidate me into resting. So we can wait if you'd like, but I'm sure."

His expression turned *hungry*, and his arms tightened reflexively around me. "Don't say that if you don't mean it," he gritted out with faltering control.

"I mean it," I whispered.

Baldric stared at me for a moment, clearly fighting himself, then his magic crashed through me with a warmth that felt like home. His triumphant roar shook the room, and I laughed in delight.

"Take me back to bed, dragon," I coaxed as his magic wove through mine, binding us together.

His eyes glinted. "There's a perfectly good sofa in here."

"So there is." I grinned, and with a spike of my magic, *all* of our clothes slid to the floor. I took a slow step back and Baldric's eyes lit with predatory intent. "And we can make use of it just as soon as you catch me."

"I'll always catch you," he promised.

"And I'll always let you," I replied with a wink.

Then, I bolted.

We both lived up to our promises.

BONUS EPILOGUE

EPILOGUE I

Ansel

Ten years later…

Feora's hand tightened on my arm as the gathered crowd glanced our way. A low rumble of displeasure built in her chest, and I instinctively pulled her closer and used my body to shield her from view.

She could protect herself, and she wasn't really in any danger here, but old habits died hard.

Feora sighed and melted into my arms. "As much as I'd love to stay here all night, they're going to want to meet you."

"I don't care what they want," I assured her.

She pressed a kiss to my jaw, and I tightened my arms around her. She'd been complaining about this summit for *months,* and now that we were here, her protective—and possessive—instincts were in turmoil. She'd warned me, of course, so I knew the best thing I could do for her was to stick close and stay in constant contact with her.

As if that were a hardship. A decade in and I still wanted her with a fierceness that stole my breath.

Dragons held a summit every twenty-five years, and this was our first time attending. Feora would've skipped it entirely, except attendance was mandatory, and any dragon who didn't appear would find themselves facing down four angry elders a short while later.

"Let's get this over with," she grumbled.

I brushed my lips over hers. "I might not be an official knight anymore, but I can still rescue a beautiful woman. Give me the word, and I'll whisk you away to our room."

She groaned and her hands tightened. "Don't tempt me."

I grinned at her. "I brought books."

Her eyes were dark enough that they appeared black in all but the brightest light, but as the heat in them grew, the truth was revealed—they were deep purple, the same color as her scales in her dragon form.

She looked dainty, my lady dragon, with delicate features and long dark hair, but she could lift a wagon full of gold like it weighed nothing at all.

And she would trade the entire wagon for a single book.

"What did you bring?" she demanded.

I grinned at her and whispered, "Come with me and I'll show you."

Her mouth opened, but a throat clearing behind us interrupted whatever she'd been about to say. She heaved another sigh, then reluctantly stepped out of my embrace while keeping a hand on my arm.

A petite redhead was giving us a knowing grin, but her own hand was clamped tightly around the arm of the tall blond woman next to her.

"Feora, introduce us to your new mate."

Feora's grip tightened, and I could feel the beginnings of a growl vibrating her chest. The other woman, who must be a dragon herself, just laughed. "I've been bonded for two centuries. Your mate is safe with me, so stop snarling and introduce us." She slanted an amused glance at the woman beside her. "They're newly mated, so tread lightly unless you want to get growled at."

Every person here was either a dragon or a dragon's bonded mate, and based on appearance alone, it was difficult to tell who was who. But there were a few couples scattered across the full room, and even between those pairs who were ancient enough to sport the first subtle signs of aging, one partner was keeping a keen eye—or hand—on the other.

Bonded mates were sacred to dragons, so I wasn't in any danger, but dragons were also possessive to a fault about anything they considered theirs.

Mates especially.

Feora huffed out a breath. "Melini, if I recall correctly, you nearly burned down our host's ballroom when he first tried to talk to your pretty new mate."

The red-haired woman's eyes narrowed. "Served him right for sneaking up on me like that." She turned her gaze to me, and her expression softened. "Don't worry, this ballroom is stone, so Feora can't burn it down. I'm Melini, and this is my mate Shalla."

I bowed slightly. "It's a pleasure. I'm Ansel."

Before Feora could fuss at me, I wrapped an arm around her and pulled her closer. She leaned into my touch with a happy little hitch in her breath that never failed to set my blood on fire. I shifted slightly and wondered just how long we needed to stay at this event that made her so nervous. Maybe I could sneak her up to our room before dinner.

The summit was supposed to last a week, but only a few of the events were truly mandatory—and tonight's dinner was not one of them.

Feora and Melini fell into conversation, and Shalla caught my gaze. She edged closer, though her mate didn't release her arm. "How long have you been mated?" she asked.

"Just over a decade."

The blonde smiled. "No wonder she's so keen to keep you away from everyone. I'd tell you it gets better, but…" She trailed off and dropped an amused glance to the delicate hand wrapped possessively around her arm. "So many dragons in one place makes them all a little nervous, but you have no reason to worry. Every dragon in here would protect you with their life. If you ever *do* get separated, it's safe to ask anyone for help. Even the surliest dragon will help a bonded mate."

She turned enough to scan the room, then tipped her head at a man leaning against the far corner. He had a circle of emptiness around him and he was clad in all black, including a hooded cloak that cast his face into shadow. "Malaki is perhaps the most dangerous dragon here, and even he helped me without complaint a few summits ago when Melini was late returning from a meeting."

Dragons had exceptional hearing, but it should've been impossible for Malaki to hear Shalla over the muted roar of conversation in the room. Still, his hooded head dipped in our direction.

I might *logically* understand that the dragon wasn't a threat, but that didn't stop me from pulling Feora closer and putting a protective hand on her waist. Malaki's hood dipped again, then he pointedly turned away.

After a few more minutes, Melini and Shalla drifted away, and Feora led me deeper into the room with a resigned grumble. She introduced me to a whirlwind of people while I kept a sharp eye out for a chance to escape.

At her hum of interest, I returned my attention to her. She was staring at a tall blond man who was icily scowling at everyone who dared to look at the pretty, dark-haired woman with him. The woman gently elbowed him with a teasing smile, but the man's scowl only deepened.

"I didn't realize Baldric had mated," Feora murmured.

My eyes narrowed at the odd note in her voice. I'd hadn't spent a decade with a dragon without learning something of possessiveness, but I kept my voice mild as I asked, "You know him?"

"He's my cousin. We were born around the same time, so we grew up together." She huffed out a soft laugh. "Or at least as together as dragons ever get. We drifted apart as the years lengthened."

My jealousy died, and I nudged her forward. "Let's go say hello."

The icy dragon's eyes raked over me before landing on Feora and warming slightly. A wry smile touched his mouth, but it didn't stop him from tugging his mate closer as we approached.

The woman at his side huffed at him. "Dragon, quit being ridiculous. I'm not going anywhere."

Baldric brushed his lips over her temple with a barely audible rumble. "I warned you, witch."

"You might've left out a few pertinent details. Like how you followed me to *the bathroom*. You're lucky I love you."

"I *am* lucky," he murmured, completely unrepentant.

We stopped just shy of what would've been the normal distance for a human conversation, and the icy dragon dipped his head at Feora. "It's good to see you, cousin."

"You, too. Congratulations on your mating."

Before Baldric could respond, his mate asked me, "Does she follow you to the bathroom?"

I glanced down at the possessive woman currently plastered to my side and grinned. "It hasn't come up yet, but I'm going to assume so."

"Damn right," Feora muttered at the same time Baldric said, "See?"

The woman's gaze flashed between us, then she smiled in relief. "Is this your first summit, too?"

"It is," I assured her. "I'm trying to figure out how to escape back to our room as soon as possible."

Her eyes widened and she glanced around as her voice lowered. "Can we *do* that?"

"I don't know, but I'm going to vanish first and ask forgiveness later. Perhaps you should do the same."

She held out her hand even as Baldric growled. "I'm Zenira, and this is Baldric, my grumpy dragon."

I had to lean forward to take her hand, but one look at Baldric's face and I decided it was better than attempting a step closer. "I'm Ansel, and this is Feora."

"A pleasure," Zenira said. Her eyes roved around the space. "So, do you think escaping at the same time would make us less inconspicuous or more?"

"You do realize half the room can hear you?" Baldric asked mildly. "And even if they couldn't, escaping a ballroom full of testy dragons unnoticed would require a miracle."

"So what you're saying," Zenira said slowly, mischief in her growing smile, "is that I don't need to be sneaky." She winked at me. "I hope I get to see you again later in the week." Then she stood on her tiptoes and whispered something in Baldric's ear. The dragon's eyes widened, then he snatched her up and began to shoulder his way through the room.

I glanced down at Feora, and she shook her head. "Don't even think—"

I scooped her up and strode toward Malaki's corner and the door I hoped led straight to the servant's staircase.

"Put me down right this instant," Feora demanded, but her arm was curled possessively around my neck and her body was relaxed. "No one abducts a dragon. It's not *done!*"

"It is now, Lady Dragon. But if it makes you feel better, I'll let you have your wicked way with me once you've been successfully abducted."

Her breath hitched and her eyes glowed with desire. "I'm going to *devour* you," she promised, her voice husky. My head emptied of all thoughts except getting her into our room and out of her clothes.

Malaki tipped his head back just enough for me to catch the tiny smirk on his lips as we passed. "Take the stairs on the left," he advised.

I bounded up the stairs two at a time. As soon as the sounds of the ballroom faded, Feora ran her hands over my chest, unlacing my tunic. Tiny claws pricked at me, proving just how much her instincts were riding her, and I groaned as my blood fled south.

By the time I found our room, Feora's hand was in my trousers, and she was slowly killing me with tiny, delicious strokes.

I had just enough sense to kick the door closed behind me, then Feora *moved*, letting go of me and vaulting from my arms with an ease that proved just how laughable the thought of abducting a dragon truly was.

Before I could do more than groan at the loss, she was there, backing me into the door and sinking down before me, her eyes blazing. My trousers fell to her claws, and her smile was pure sin.

"*Mine*," she growled.

"Yours," I agreed with a gasp as her hands slid up my thighs. Then there was no thinking at all because the heat of her mouth wrapped around the head of my cock. Her tongue stroked me and I was lost. My head fell back against the door with a moan, and I held onto control by the thinnest threads as she slowly unraveled me.

A pleased growl rumbled through her and my eyes crossed in bliss. "Feora," I gasped, reaching blindly for her, "let me——"

The growl deepened as she took me to the hilt, and the combination was too much. White-hot lightning bolted through me, and I came with a shout that they likely heard back in the ballroom.

When I could see again, I found Feora smiling up at me, looking both pleased and smug. I gently touched her cheek, awed yet again that she had chosen me. "I love you," I whispered. I would never get tired of the way the words made her eyes glow with pleasure, no matter how many times a day I told her.

"I love you, too," she replied. Then she licked her lips. "But I believe I promised to *devour* you. This was a nice appetizer, but I think we can do better."

"Any better and you might kill me," I admitted.

Her grin was not reassuring, so I bent and lifted her before she could follow through. I tossed her onto the bed and she landed with a laugh. "My turn," I growled playfully.

She sent me a challenging look through her lashes. "If you think you're up for it."

I laughed darkly. The dragon magic coursing through my veins meant my refractory period was unbelievably short, something she very well knew. "You're going to regret taunting me, Lady Dragon."

Her lips curved into a wicked smile. "Promise?"

Rather than answering, I slowly pulled my tunic over my head, flexing the muscles I'd spent years honing. Feora's breath hitched and I smiled.

I crawled onto the bed, stalking my dragon in the way that made her shiver and moan without a single touch. I sat back on my knees and gave my thickening cock a lazy stroke while Feora's eyes remained glued to me.

"You're wearing too many clothes. Let me help." I skimmed my hands over her legs, barely touching, as I unfastened her trousers and removed them and the layer underneath, leaving her bare from the waist down.

When I stared at her and licked my lips, her breath stilled and her hands curled into fists. But rather than burying my face between her delicious thighs, I started on the buttons of her blouse. *Slowly.* By the time she was naked, we were both breathing hard.

"Ansel." My name was a prayer and a plea.

I dipped my head and kissed her, unable to resist tasting her. She hooked her legs over my hips and arched her back, trying to hurry me along. I nipped her jaw, and she growled at me.

Her instincts were too close to the surface for too much teasing, but I'd promised her retribution. I slid down, pausing only to suck a taut, pretty nipple into my mouth for a moment before continuing. She spread her legs around my shoulders with a moan.

She was slick and molten, and I groaned as my cock throbbed, desperate to feel that heat. At the first touch of my tongue, she arched and hissed out, "Yessss."

I feasted like a man starving as she buried her claw-tipped fingers in my hair. I could stay here for hours, but today she needed hard and fast. I drove her ruthlessly toward her peak until she shattered on my tongue, then I surged up and buried my cock in her throbbing heat.

"Mine," I growled, meeting her eyes.

She clenched around me and pleasure burned up my spine. But her stubborn little mouth remained shut, her expression challenging.

I sat back and dragged her hips with me, so I could thumb her clit with every thrust. "You're mine, Lady Dragon," I murmured, giving her pleasure and reassurance in equal measure. "Mine to care for."

Her body clenched again, and her eyes glowed brighter.

"Mine to *fuck*."

She moaned and her hips lifted.

"Mine to love."

The fiery burn of pleasure was nearly impossible to ignore, but she was wound tight, her muscles fluttering around my cock.

"Mine," I demanded again, my thumb stroking her exactly how she preferred.

"Yours!" she finally wailed as she came.

The pleasure compressed into a single, infinite point before exploding outward, tipping me over the edge. I buried myself deep and let go, joining her in bliss. I collapsed forward, putting us skin to skin. For all that Feora looked delicate, I knew I wouldn't crush her.

She cuddled into me, wrapping her arms around my back and caressing the slick skin over my shoulder blades. "I love you," she whispered.

I smiled against her throat. "I'm aware."

She swatted at me with a laugh. "And I'm sorry I'm a little out of control." She shivered. "There are too many threats here, even though I logically know they're not threats."

I heaved myself up onto my elbow so I could meet her eyes. "I don't mind. Whatever you need, I'm here."

Mischief flitted across her face before she flipped us. "In that case…"

We missed dinner.

Neither of us minded.

EPILOGUE 2

Baldric

The quarter-century summits were a necessary evil, but that didn't mean I was happy to be here. It had been bad enough before I'd met Zenira, but now that she was at my side, my instincts demanded that I hide her away and keep her safe.

Instincts didn't care that the other attendees weren't a threat and that even if they *were*, Zenira could take care of herself. She would always be mine to protect. Dragons who'd been mated for less than a century got a lot of leeway during the summit.

Even so, we had to leave our room *sometimes*, and I hated it every damn time.

Zenira, however, *loved* meeting the other dragons and bonded mates. I could refuse her nothing, so I clenched my jaw and glued myself to her side. On the first day, she'd teased me about following her to the bathroom, but I couldn't have pried myself away if I'd *wanted* to—and I didn't.

We'd made it through half the week and my control was

faltering. There were too many threats, too many people, and the desire to *snatch* and *hoard* and *protect* was nearly irresistible.

Zenira chattered happily as she changed into a dress for dinner, and I breathed in her warm scent. She smelled like cozy fires and warm bread and happiness—in a word, she smelled like *home*.

And I had to share her yet again with everyone else. If I made it through the evening without bloodshed, I'd count it as a win.

I snagged her arm as she fluttered past and drew her close. I nuzzled her temple and fought for control.

"This is really getting to you, huh?" she asked quietly.

"Dragons are solitary for a reason. So many of us together, is… uncomfortable."

She nestled deeper into my arms and some of my roaring anxiety calmed. She was here and safe and mine.

As if she heard my thoughts, she murmured, "You know I'm not going anywhere, right? You're stuck with me, I'm afraid."

I ran a grateful hand down her back. "I know, but it doesn't matter. You'll always be precious to me, and I'll always want to keep you safe."

She pressed a kiss to my jaw, then grinned at me and wiggled her fingers. "Want me to drive them all away?"

"I would like nothing more," I told her honestly, "but it would lead to other problems. I will survive." *Probably.*

Her brows drew together, but before she could offer to skip dinner—an offer I would be hard pressed to refuse—I brushed my lips across hers. She made a little sound of pleasure and wound her arms around my neck, pressing closer.

She glided her tongue over my bottom lip, then sucked it into the heat of her mouth. I groaned and clutched her tighter. If I lifted the silken fabric of her dress and buried my face between her legs, she would forget all about dinner.

She would stay here, with me.

And miss out on an evening of socializing. I might hate it, but *she* didn't, and it wasn't often that she got to meet so many other people with magic. I'd already stolen her away more than I should've, but she'd never once complained.

I broke the kiss but couldn't quite force myself to let her go entirely. "Are you finished getting ready?"

She blinked up at me, then nodded. Her cheeks were flushed and her lips glistened and she was the most beautiful thing I'd ever seen. I kissed her again, unable to resist, and she moaned into my mouth before reaching down to stroke me through my trousers.

My fractured control snapped.

I spun her around and clamped her back to my chest. I cupped her breast and rolled her tight nipple between my fingers, drawing another moan from her. "We don't have much time, so we'll have to be fast. Will you be fast for me?"

She nodded furiously with another low sound of pleasure, and I dragged her skirt and chemise up only to find the minx wasn't wearing anything else. I instantly went harder than stone. I buried my growl against her neck and fought for restraint.

She reached back and wove her hands in my hair, arching her spine and rubbing against my aching cock. "I thought you might like that," she murmured. "I was going to surprise you after dinner." She peeked at me over her shoulder, and her smile was pure wickedness. "Or maybe *at* dinner."

My hands clenched. "Witch."

"Dragon." She was unrepentant, glowing with desire and love.

I let go of her clothes and turned us until we faced the mirrored dressing table, then I guided her hands down to the edge. She met my eyes in the mirror and slowly licked her lips.

I unfastened my trousers, then dragged her dress back up. Her breath caught as I ran my hands over the sweet curve of her ass. I dipped my fingers between her legs and she lifted onto her toes with a gasp.

She was slick and already quivering. I nudged her legs farther apart, then took myself in hand and sank into her heat in excruciatingly tiny increments. She was as tight as a fist in this position, and despite her wiggling insistence that I hurry, I would never risk hurting her.

Once I was fully seated, she collapsed to her elbows with a low moan and the change caused my breath to hiss out on a curse.

"I love the way you feel like this," she whispered. She pushed up enough to shift forward before rocking back, fucking herself on my cock.

I groaned and clenched her hips, stilling her. "You had your fun this afternoon. It's my turn."

Before she could complain, I moved, giving her the short, hard thrusts she preferred in this position. Her breathing turned ragged and her eyes squeezed closed as the pleasure built.

Aware that we were already late, I only kept her balanced on the edge for a few precious minutes before driving her past the point of no return. Her body locked and pulsed around me.

Pleasure hit like a hammer, and I roared my claim so all would know she was mine.

Zenira chuckled breathlessly. "So much for being discreet."

I pressed a kiss to the damp nape of her neck. "Dragons have sharp noses. We could've been as quiet as mice and they would still know."

A blush deepened the color in her cheeks, but there was interest there, too. "So every time we…?"

"Yes."

A slow, possessive smile curved over her lips. "Good. That way none of them will doubt you're mine."

~

THE BANQUET HALL was filled with long tables draped in pristine white cloth. Seating was not assigned, and nearly all of the seats were already filled by the time we arrived, but there were two chairs available across from Feora and Ansel.

I wasn't the only one who'd noticed Zenira enjoyed chatting with them, and gratitude unknotted some of my lingering tension.

I helped Zenira into her seat, then sat across from Feora with a subtle grimace. Her lips twisted in sympathy, then she took a breath and her smile turned amused, as if her mate hadn't been drowning in her scent all week.

We were at the end of the table, so as long as the seat at the foot of the table remained empty, I'd have a small buffer between Zenira and the rest of the room. Thanks to our pleasurable delay, I was feeling a little less frayed than I had been. Maybe this dinner wouldn't be so bad.

The universe, however, was not on my side. Just as a server placed a bowl of soup in front of me, a dark cloud descended on the empty chair.

Zenira thanked the server, then tilted her head at the dragon dressed in black who'd just sat far too close to her. It was all I could do not to snatch her into the safety of my arms. Feora's hands were fisted on the table, her lip curled.

My witch, however, was fearless. She beamed at the newcomer. "Welcome to our table. I'm Zenira. I don't think we've met..." She trailed off, waiting for Malaki to offer his name.

Malaki's hood shadowed his face, but shadows alone couldn't hide him from dragon eyes, and he wasn't using his magic. Surprise crossed his face for an instant before he dipped his head at Zenira. "I'm Malaki."

He glanced at me and Feora. "Peace," he murmured, low enough that the humans likely couldn't hear him. "I mean no harm."

"Nice to meet you," Zenira said. She hooked her leg around mine, and I realized I was slowly crushing my wine goblet. She touched the goblet, fixing it with her magic, then continued as if nothing was amiss. "You probably know Baldric and Feora already, but that's Ansel, Feora's mate."

Malaki nodded to Ansel.

"This is our first summit."

Malaki nodded again, but didn't respond. Zenira smiled softly at him, then turned her attention to Ansel. "Have you seen the glasshouse arboretum yet?"

Ansel glanced at Feora, and his smile was the tiniest bit playful. "We explored it yesterday." His gaze returned to Zenira. "Gorgeous, isn't it?"

"Yes! I went today while Baldric was in that interminable meeting." Her eyes slid down my body like a caress. "It's a maze, but he didn't have any trouble finding me."

I could find her anywhere on the grounds, and not just because she'd pilfered one of my rocks. She wore it on a necklace, a talisman just for me. The small magical prickle I felt at having a rock outside of my hoard was more than made up for the fact that I could find her anywhere in the world.

But here, I didn't need that sort of magic. I could track her scent through any of the nearby buildings, which I had done just as soon as I'd been released from the latest round of discussions.

My witch had a naughty streak, and she'd led me into the fragile privacy of one of the glasshouse's many hidden nooks before laying me bare in more ways than one.

Most dragons cared little about modesty, and Zenira and I hadn't been the only ones who'd had a pleasant afternoon in the humid warmth of the glasshouse. When I'd warned her she needed to be quiet or risk being overheard, she'd flushed down to her chest and clenched around me tight enough to make me see stars.

Zenira and Ansel chatted while Feora and I kept a close eye

on Malaki. Even together we'd be no match for him, but every dragon here would turn on him if he tried anything with another's bonded mate.

But while Malaki was stony and standoffish, he'd never been anything but carefully polite with the few mates who had braved his forbidding presence.

It was cold comfort when the threat sat nearly within reach.

Zenira's leg jostled mine, and she looked at me expectantly. I replayed the last few minutes of conversation, aware that I'd been paying more attention to our surroundings than the table.

"There's a Knights & Bandits board in the library, if I recall correctly." I slanted a glance at Ansel. "But don't be fooled by her innocent face. Zenira is dangerously good."

She elbowed me in the side with an exaggerated scowl. "Stop giving away all of my secrets." She tipped her head toward Malaki. "Do you play?"

His hood dipped slightly, and Zenira, being who she was, invited, "Would you like to join us for a game?"

Malaki's gaze flickered over Feora and me, and one corner of his lips pulled up into the shadow of a smile. "Thank you, but no."

THE REST of dinner passed peacefully enough, but it was a relief to usher Zenira into the empty library. Feora and Ansel followed us, and while Feora's presence still made me want to bare my teeth, we had grown up together so the impulse was less pressing than it would've been with another dragon.

Through unspoken agreement, Feora and I herded Ansel and Zenira into a protected corner with a quartet of cushioned chairs arranged around a low table. High shelves blocked the rest of the room. Based on Zenira's smile and Ansel's far too innocent look, neither of them was unaware of what we were doing.

Feora left just long enough to retrieve the Knights & Bandits board—after giving me a glare that promised a slow death if I so much as looked at Ansel while she was gone.

While Zenira set up the board and reminded Ansel of the rules, Feora relaxed enough to join me by the sole entrance to the corner. She blew out a slow breath. "I'm ready for this week to be over."

"You and me both."

Her smile was small and wry. "I owe a lot of mated dragons apologies for thinking they were too overprotective during the previous summits."

"At least you didn't singe off anyone's eyebrows. Remember Harold's first summit with his mate?"

She chuckled. "His mate looked like he couldn't decide whether to scold Harold for overreacting or to jump him right there in the hall."

"Now that I think about it, Harold might've had the right idea. The others *still* give them a wide berth, and that was three centuries ago."

When her expression turned contemplative, I chuckled. "Don't do something that will make your mate fuss at you. We only have a few more days to survive, then we can all retreat and recover until the next one."

Feora grimaced, then grumbled, "Ansel would like to visit you and Zenira. Or have you visit us. He's starting to realize he's going to outlive his family, and it's... *difficult* for him. He loves people so easily, and it would be nice if he had friends who were going to stick around."

I bit back my instinctive denial, then groaned and cursed. I ran a reluctant hand down my face and begrudgingly admitted, "Zenira would love that, too."

Feora's expression was appropriately sympathetic, but a tiny smile played over her lips as she glanced at Ansel. "The things we do for our mates."

I studied Zenira's beaming smile as she took one of Ansel's pieces, and the last of my resistance melted away. "Indeed."

Together, we stared at the most precious people in our worlds and quietly made plans to keep them happy for the rest of our long, long lives.

About the Author

Jessie Mihalik has a degree in Computer Science and a love of all things geeky. A software engineer by trade, Jessie now writes full time from her home in Texas. When she's not writing, she can be found playing co-op video games with her husband, trying out new board games, or reading books pulled from her overflowing bookshelves.

CONNECT WITH JESSIE:

www.jessiemihalik.com
Twitter: @jessiemihalik
Facebook: /JessMihalik
Instagram: @jessmihalik

Want all of the latest book news, info, and snippets delivered straight to your inbox? Sign up for Jessie's newsletter!
https://www.jessiemihalik.com/newsletter/

www.ingramcontent.com/pod-product-compliance
Lightning Source LLC
Chambersburg PA
CBHW050405110726
47899CB00008B/2663